Amiens Song 7

1 *How They Lived In The Greenwood* 9

2 *The Tale of Little John* 12

3 *The Tale of Will Scarlet* 18

4 *The Greenwood Code* 25

5 *Robin Hood's Inn* 31

6 *Robin and the Bishop* 43

7 *The Defenders of Gamwell Hall* 53

8 *The Tale of Friar Tuck* 58

9 *The Tale of Alan-a-Dale* 66

10 *How Robin Sold Pots at Nottingham Fair* 72

11 *The Black Monks* 86

12 *The Two Strong Wills* 92

13 *The Rescuing of the Widow's Three Sons* 97

14 *Little John's Adventure* 109

15 *Vengeance on Guy of Gisborne* 115

16 *Capture and Escape* 122

17 *A Greenwood Wedding* 129

18 *The Coming of Richard the King* 134

19 *Robin Hood at the Court of King Richard* 143

20 *Robin's Return to the Greenwood* 146

21 *Robin's Death and Burial* 151

Under the greenwood tree
Who loves to lie with me,
And tune his merry note
Unto the sweet bird's throat,
Come hither, come hither, come hither:
Here shall me see
No enemy
But winter and rough weather.

—Amiens Song.

1

How They Lived In The Greenwood

In the joyous olden days of Merrie England, there dwelt in the green glades of Sherwood Forest, in the County of Nottinghamshire, a band of merry men. Outlaws, the rich folk called them; fellows who lived a wild roving life, caring nothing for the protection of King or State which other sober folk enjoyed, owning no master but one who was as wild, as roving, as lawless, as the rest of them—a clever, freakish fellow, whose name was Robin Hood.

'Twas whispered that once he had been a great man, owning broad lands and fine houses in the fair country of England. But ill luck, or—to twist matters about—as he himself said, good fortune, had taught him to care more for his trusty bow and arrow than all the riches in the world. And he found at last that dainty food, soft beds, and a house roof to cover him seemed but a poor exchange for the flesh of the deer he had hunted and killed, the dew-laden berries of the woods, the forest grass that was his resting-place at night, and, over his head, naught but the spreading branches of the greenwood trees he loved, to come between him and the stars.

And many men, who seemed to be of the same mind as he, found their home with him in the woodlands, and took him for their leader. Odd fellows they were, coming one scarcely knew whence, but all hardy, strong, and fearless; skilful in the use of bow and arrow, careless and free, and with a mighty love of the greenwood and the life they led therein.

There was Little John, the long-limbed young giant whom Robin Hood loved as a brother; there was Will Scarlet, the finest hunter of deer; Alan-a-Dale, who sang his comrades ballads at eventide when the day's adventures were done, and whose voice was as sweet and joyous as a lark's on a May morning. There was Midge, the miller's mighty son, and Friar Tuck, who had left his cloister and his abbot for the Sherwood oaks and the merry forest-life lived by Robin and his men. All these there were and many more, who would not have exchanged their free way of living for all the broad lands of the kingdom, for the very crown of the King himself.

From dawn to dark Robin Hood's men, in their coats of Lincoln green, were astir in the greenwood, hunting the King's deer, up and down the glades that every man knew as well as he knew his own face in the forest pools; seeking adventures upon the King's highways; lightening the King's rich nobles of their too heavy purses; helping and comforting the King's poor subjects in their hour of need.

For though the King's wealthy lords fumed and fretted at Robin Hood's doings, and swore that he and all his robber-rogues should be caught and hung without delay, yet the poor folk knew that in Robin Hood, the outlaw, they had a staunch friend. Proud knights, and bishops, and abbots, lordlings and high sheriffs—all these, met upon the high roads by Robin Hood's green-coated followers, would be relieved of their wealth and jewels with a laughing: "By your leave, fair sir! My master bids ye pay a visit with us to Robin Hood's Inn!" And, willy-nilly, lordling, or knight, or abbot, was forced to go, for those men in green, bristling with bows and arrows, swarmed all around and up and out of the greenwood, as if they had been indeed the forest's own children.

But for the poor folk—for labourers and old men, yeomen and squires, knights whose lands had been taken from them by grasping nobles, women and little children, Robin and his men had naught but fair words and always a ready hand to help where help was needed. And these people knew that they were free to come and go as they cared, fearing nothing, for those greenwood lads were careful only to take toll from the rich and the proud.

So the days and the years spent in Sherwood Forest passed by merrily, and many an adventure had Robin Hood and the men in green.

And the stories of these adventures—gallant and grave—have been left to us by the minstrels in old rhymes and legends, so that we in England know well today how they lived in the greenwood in days gone by.

For tales such as these never grew old or dull in the telling; and now you, children of England, may hear them once again, and remember that this country's history is all the brighter and better because once there lived in England a gallant, true-hearted outlaw, whose name was Robin Hood.

2

The Tale of Little John

In his new suit of Lincoln green, Robin strolled round the outlaw camp in Sherwood Forest. He watched his men preparing arrows, refixing bow strings, and carrying out sundry repairs to their weapons.

"They look as if they are fresh from battle," mused Robin to himself. "Yet for two weeks little has happened in the way of adventure."

Robin felt restless about the future. He spoke to Midge-the-Miller's son, one of the new members of the band.

"It's all very well to be the leader of so fine a band of men—and the band is still growing—but what's the use of trained fighting men if you can give them no work to do?"

The burly miller's son laid his hand on his leader's arm.

"Don't worry, master," he said. "We are contented. After all, this is the life we chose."

But Robin Hood was restless, thirsty for action.

"It's no good waiting here in the forest for some adventure to come along. It's getting dull here. I must go outside and look for something more exciting."

He set out later in the day, alone. He reminded his men to keep their ears sharpened for the call of his horn should there be trouble.

Through the greenwood he wandered, making his way over tangled undergrowth until he came to one of the shady forest paths. Along the path, aimlessly, he walked, until he came to a second path that led across the fields to a distant village.

To his left ran a stream, and he followed it for some way as it threaded a wavy course through the fields. Presently he came to a roughly-made wooden bridge. He mounted the bridge, but there he came to a sudden halt. Standing at the opposite end of the bridge was a giant of a man. He had started to cross at the same time as the outlaw.

Robin walked along the bridge to where the stranger stood. The giant made no attempt to let him pass. Instead he stood squarely in the middle of the bridge and glared insolently at Robin, as if daring him to try to pass.

Here was a situation that promised some excitement. Robin laughed merrily. It was clear that the stranger had no intention of letting him pass. Yet one of them must retreat before the other could cross—and Robin Hood, leader of the Sherwood Forest outlaws, had no intention of giving way to a stranger, however big he might be.

Robin glanced at the swirling stream below. His mind was made up.

"Let me pass, fellow!" he commanded.

The huge man did not move.

"If you don't move out of my way, you great oaf, I shall have to move you myself!" cried Robin.

The fellow only grinned. Robin became infuriated. He unslung his bow.

"If you don't move," he warned, "I'll show you how we deal with fellows like you."

As Robin fitted an arrow to his bow, the giant lumbered forward towards him. Poised in his hands was a quarter-staff.

"If you dare pull back the string," he said, grimly, "I'll dust the hide off you before you know it!"

They were brave words, for Robin, with his bow, had the advantage. Robin could have killed him if he had chosen. There was no denying this huge fellow's courage as he stared scornfully at the threatening bow. Robin admired his spirit. The outlaw backed slightly to the end of the footbridge, still with his arrow pointing certain death at the stranger.

"Your talk is foolish," said he. "I could send an arrow through your heart in quicker time than it would take to tell."

"You are a coward!" exclaimed the other, with scorn in his voice. "You are armed with bow and arrows; I have only my stout staff."

"Coward!" laughed Robin. "I like that! I'll soon show you that I am no coward."

Robin leapt off the bridge and, going to a nearby oak tree, sprang at one of the branches. By sheer force he tore it down. Quickly he stripped off the leaves and ran back to the bridge.

In the middle of the bridge the two men met. They lunged with their staves. Robin got in a blow on the giant's shoulder. Fighting back, the man hit Robin on the head with his staff. The fight grew furious. The two were well matched, for Robin was a practised fighter, and the stranger was enormously strong.

Robin poured in a shower of blows, thick and fast. The stranger smote back with a will. Then, just as Robin was beginning to think he was getting the upper hand, he missed his footing and fell with a great splash into the brook.

He struggled to the surface. Heavy rains had swollen the stream, and in the middle it was deep.

"Ho! Where are you now, my fine fellow?" laughed the stranger.

Robin spluttered from the water: "I'm in the flood You proved yourself the better man that time."

"All right!" answered the other. "So long as yo know you're beaten, I'll let you cross the bridge."

Robin waded out, lower down the stream. He wa muddy and wet. He came up to the stranger, and aske him what his business was and whether he had wor to do. The giant shook his head.

"Nobody within miles will give John Little even day's work," he said. "They're all afraid to emplo me. The trouble is that I like to work in my own wa They all want me to work in their way. But nobod ever made John Little do what he didn't want to do— so it always ends in a fight and I have to wander or often hungry. I could eat a good meal now!"

While the giant was speaking, Robin had been try ing to wash some of the mud from his new suit c Lincoln green.

"Come back with me," he said, picking up his bo and arrows. "I'll show you a band of fine fellows wh would be glad to give you a good meal."

He turned back the same way as he had come, th stranger striding after him.

As the two reached Sherwood Forest, Robin grasped his horn and placed it to his lips. His only answer was a stream of dirty water that still lay in the instrument after its soaking in the brook. Robin laughed merrily, and his companion joined in.

Robin shook the horn dry and blew again. Three loud notes rang out through the greenwood. Other horns quickly answered his call, and soon a crowd of men, dressed like himself in Lincoln green, surrounded them.

Robin gazed at them proudly.

"These are my merry men, John Little," he said. "And this," he continued, turning to his men, "is a man who would not let me pass across a bridge this morning, and instead tumbled me into a stream. What shall we do with him?"

"Duck him!" they cried. "Throw him into a stream as you were thrown!"

"No!" answered Robin. "He has proved himself a fighter with a staff. He had far better join us." He turned to the giant. "Come, join my merry band!" he said. "We have plenty to eat and drink, and as for the work we have to do—well, our work is to 'right the wrong'! If there is a tyrant anywhere about, or if a man robs the poor, he has to settle with us. There will be plenty of fighting. It is a hard life, but it offers fine sport. What say you?"

John Little was keen to join. The band turned back towards their camp, and when they reached it Robin Hood, winking mischievously, said to his merry men: "We shall have to re-christen him!"

The men laughed, and swarmed about John Little,

dragging him down to the ground. Will-the-Wrestler suggested a new name.

"He says he's John Little. Then let us call him 'Little John'!"

They poured mugfuls of water over the giant, and he became 'Little John' from that day forward. They dressed him in their uniform of Lincoln green. They taught him to shoot, and how to use his sword and dagger. He never knew again what it was to be hungry, for Robin Hood and his merry band of outlaws dined richly off the King's deer, which they shot in their forest home.

Little John grew steadily in favour with the outlaws. His rough ways were understood by all, and he became a great favourite. Robin often left him in charge of the band while he went off by himself. The men respected the giant, whose strength was enormous, and they were satisfied to have one so brave and strong as their leader when Robin was away.

3

The Tale of Will Scarlet

"It's a wonderful morning!"

Robin prodded Little John in the ribs as he spoke. The giant was still asleep under the greenwood tree. He opened his eyes as he heard Robin's voice, and, stretching his great limbs, he rose to his feet.

"You're up early," he said to Robin. The sun was only just creeping up over the horizon, but already it was sending warm beams of yellow through the gently swaying branches overhead.

Robin set out alone into the forest, where the graceful greenery of the overhanging boughs, with the sun's first rays shining down on the leafy carpet, touched his face like friendly fingers. He longed to see Maid Marian again, and to hear her merry laughter. He loved the comradeship of his Merrie Men, but he never forgot the friendship of his earlier days. It was this longing for old faces that had set him wandering, on this particular morning, alone along the forest paths.

He had reached the edge of the forest along the Nottingham road when he suddenly caught sight of a young man who evidently belonged to some good family. His doublet was all of silk; his stockings were bright scarlet.

"What a bright contrast he makes to the soft greens

and browns of the woodland," thought Robin. "And what a conspicuous target he'd make if anyone were chasing him!"

Then Robin stopped dead in his tracks.

"Hello!" he murmured to himself. "This fellow is up to something."

The man in scarlet was standing still, his eyes fixed on a herd of deer that, unaware of his presence, were grazing some distance away.

The young man spoke. His voice was soft and cultured.

"I'll have the best of you for my meal today, and very quickly, too!"

"Heavens!" exclaimed Robin under his breath, as he watched the young man fit an arrow to his bow and take steady aim.

Everyone knew that it was a very serious crime to kill the King's deer. The outlaws had been doing it for a long time, but this respectable young man was not an outlaw.

Robin stood silent as he saw the man pull back the arrow in the bow. The archer was almost forty yards away from the nearest wanderer from the herd, but, in spite of the distance, his arrow sped straight to its mark, and the stricken deer dropped where it stood, shot through the heart, while the rest of the animals scampered away in a panic.

"Well done! Well hit!" cried Robin loudly.

The young man in the scarlet stockings jumped in surprise. He was startled at the voice so near him. He thought at first that Robin must be one of the foresters of the place. If that were so, he knew that he had been caught red-handed in a crime sufficient to hang him. He had no wish to feel the noose around his neck. It would be better, he thought, to be the attacking party than to be the party attacked.

He acted at once.

"A second shot can be as good as the first," he cried as he took a step towards Robin, fitting a second arrow to his bow. "If you don't clear off, this will find a target in your ribs."

Robin did not move. Though the other was covering him menacingly with his bow and arrow, the outlaw remained fearlessly watching him. There stood the two men, facing each other. Both were unafraid, and each was waiting for the other to make a move.

Robin's face broke into a smile.

"I say again," he laughed, "well done! To bring down a deer at forty yards is the feat of a true marksman."

Suddenly the other man dropped his bow and made towards Robin with clenched fists, exclaiming: "If you don't take your carcase out of the way, I'll make you sorry that you ever saw me! What has it to do with you if I kill a deer? Answer me that!"

Robin grinned at the stranger's wrath.

"If you are so put out with a man who does nothing but pay you a compliment, what kind of a wild beast would you be to one who insulted you?"

"Drop your banter and fight me!" exclaimed the other.

"I'm willing enough to fight," returned Robin. "I love fighting for its own sake; but why should I fight you? I don't waste my time on every ill-mannered varlet who crosses my path. When I fight it is with someone of much finer mettle than you!"

Robin's tone was not bitter. It was gently sarcastic. He knew well that his mockery would not help to bring about peace.

"Boasts, mere boasts!" fumed the other.

He rushed to his bow once more to finish the argument and to avenge the insults. But, as he turned, he found that he was already covered by Robin, who had drawn his bow more quickly.

"Now," cried Robin, the smile that had been playing about his lips vanishing, "move but one step and I send this arrow flying towards you! If you want a fight, you have a sword by your side. So have I. You are obviously the son of a good family and are entitled to wear a sword. Unsheathe your blade, then, and I'll cross swords with you!"

The young man wanted no further prompting. He drew his blade immediately and there followed a clashing of steel as sword met sword.

They had not been fighting long before Robin realised that his opponent was no mean fighter. This man was a fine swordsman and Robin had hard work defending himself. Practised as he was in every feint and pass and thrust, Robin discovered that the young man was ready for him and that he must fence with all the tricks and skill he possessed, or his own defence would be broken through.

"This is just the man for my band," said Robin to himself as they fought on, breathlessly. "A brave fellow, and skilled with his bow as well as with his sword. He's the very man for me. But, first, I must win this contest."

He pressed the stranger hard, and the other replied with fresh zeal. The clash of shining steel rang out through the forest as the two fought desperately. First Robin would drive his opponent back; then, under a renewed onslaught, he would give ground before a series of fierce thrusts.

It was not long, however, before Robin could see that his opponent was losing strength. The outlaw knew that by attacking even more fiercely, the stranger would be compelled to give in. Robin closed in with renewed energy. He flashed around the young man, bringing into play all his skill and daring. It was too much for his brave opponent. Slowly he gave way. He was being worn down.

With one terrific stroke, Robin crashed the other's sword from his hand. The stranger was completely at his mercy—and he knew it! But Robin had no wish to harm him. Instead, he dropped his own sword.

"Listen to me!" said he. "You are a tough lad, whoever you are. You should have a mind for a life of adventure."

"That's why I am here," exclaimed the other, recovering his breath. "I set out to join the band of Robin Hood."

"Oh! Did you?" smiled Robin.

It was going to be easy to persuade this young man to join him!

"But why should you want to join him?" bantered Robin. "Don't you know that every man's hand is turned against him? He is an outlaw, you know!"

"I do know. And my hand isn't turned against him, for one!" was the reply. "Tales of his adventures have spread far and wide. People who know him have described him to me. He—why, now I come to think of it, he is something like you to look at!"

"I am he!" said Robin.

"You!" The other was nonplussed, not knowing what to say.

Robin dropped his sword into its sheath. "It's strange that we should meet in this way. I must take you to my men. They will be pleased to see you. But, tell me, why did you leave your home? What have you done?"

"Well, to tell you the truth," explained the other, "I had an accident, in which I nearly killed one of my father's servants. It is not yet known whether the man will live or die."

"Hm!" mused Robin. "That may be serious."

"Yes, that's just the trouble. If he lives, everything will be all right. If he dies, you know what will happen to me if I am caught."

"You'll be dangling on the end of a rope."

"I thought the only thing to do," went on the stranger, "was to join you in the life I have heard about ever since you fled from the Sheriff of Nottingham. I ran away while I was still free and came straight here."

"Good," said the outlaw leader. "If you like adventure, we shall not disappoint you. I'll lead you to my men, and they will treat you as one of themselves."

His eyes twinkled as he spoke. It was a custom with his men to re-christen all new members. Robin had already thought of a new name for this man.

The two had been walking for some distance when they came to a glade. Here Robin blew the well-known call on his horn. Soon, men came running through the forest to him. They stopped short when they saw the strong young stranger in scarlet stockings.

"Men," called Robin, as his band eyed the newcomer, "I want you to meet a new member. He has come to join our band and to be one of us. Make him welcome—and see that he is well fed."

The men made him welcome for Robin's sake. They gave him some of their own meal and made a special feast of it in his honour.

"Now for the christening!" announced Midge-the-Miller's son, when the meal was over.

"What are we to call him?" asked Will-the-Wrestler.

The outlaws were silent for a moment. Then, "What name are you known by?" asked Little John.

"I was christened—that is, first christened—William," said the youth, eyeing the preparations for his second christening curiously.

"But we cannot call him William," said Little John, "for sometimes that's what we call Will-the-Wrestler."

The outlaws suggested various names, but none could think of a suitable name for the stranger. Robin helped them out of the difficulty.

"Look at his stockings!" he laughed. "Finer scarlet never graced a young man's leg. He shall be called Will Scarlet."

The christening ceremony was carried out in front of the trestle tables. Will Scarlet was made a member of Robin Hood's band—a valuable member, who became one of Robin's right-hand men.

4

The Greenwood Code

Passing one day through Sherwood Forest, a traveller was ambushed and captured by Robin Hood's men. His hands were roughly thrust behind him, and tied tightly.

"Well done!" said Little John. "We will take the fellow to Robin Hood."

They made their way through the forest, the traveller with his bundles and his horse going in front of them.

Robin Hood was angry when he examined the traveller.

"Who tied this man's hands behind him in this ruthless manner?" he demanded, turning upon his men.

They looked at each other in surprise. Then Little John said: "I did it! And I thought it very well done!"

"You did!" said Robin, angrily. "I can see you did!" He turned to his men. "Seize Little John and tie him up in the same way!"

Despite his struggles, the giant was overpowered, and his hands were tied tightly behind his back, as he had tied those of the traveller. His bonds cut deeply into his wrists. But the outlaws, though they did as they were told, could not understand their leader's purpose. There were some black looks for him from a number of his band. The looks were noted by Robin. He turned to Little John and said: "Now, how do you like it yourself? Was it necessary to tie the captive's hands so tightly? It is unpleasant enough to be taken captive without adding to a man's discomfort. Never tie too tightly, or I shall tie you! Don't handle people too roughly, or I shall see that you no longer remain men of my band. I want strong men, it is true, but they must also be men of gentle hearts."

Robin spoke directly to Little John.

"You have had your lesson, and now you shall be freed, Little John. You and I know each other well, and you will understand my rough handling. I did it to show the rest how we must take prisoners."

When his thongs were removed Little John looked ruefully at his wrists. He turned to the prisoner.

"I did not realise that I had tied you so tightly," he said. "Pray forgive me."

"Very handsomely said!" exclaimed Robin. "And now"—turning to the captive traveller—"sit down on the grass and tell us where you were taking your goods, and from where you came."

His bonds cut, the man sat down.

"This morning," he began, "as the sun rose in the heavens, I set forth from Nottingham with my goods. You will see that I am only a young man. I have not been in business long, and in Nottingham I found it was slow work waiting for customers to come to me. So I decided to pack my horse with some of my coarser cloth and travel to the villages. I thought that I might be able to sell some cloth to the labourers and their women."

"But as I wandered along the forest path, your men surprised me and brought me here. It is a great pity that I did not know beforehand that I should fall into your hands, for I should certainly have brought some Lincoln-green cloth with me to sell to you."

Robin and his men burst out laughing at the way in which this man seemed to take for granted that he had missed a bargain.

"Then you were not travelling to sell some fine dainty cloths to the squires of the district and their ladies?" queried Robin.

"Certainly not," said the man. "Had I done so they might have taken what they wanted and left me to find the money as best I could; for we live in a time when might is right."

Robin nodded; he knew too well that this was the truth. He turned to his men.

"Open his pack," he said, "and if he has spoken the truth about his travelling to sell to honest poor folk he shall go on his way unmolested."

The pack was opened and it contained, as the traveller had claimed, bales of russet browns, and cloth of grey and drab, such as common folk would wear; but there was no cloth that any knight or dame or squire or lady would have dreamed of wearing.

"The man has spoken the truth!" declared Robin. "We have no wish to wage war upon the poor, and we don't want to spoil their chances of making an honest living. Let us, then, allow this man to go free. What do you say, men?"

The outlaws broke out into loud applause, and the traveller felt relieved to think that he was now a free man.

"I will ride this way again," he said, "and when I do I will bring with me some bales of Lincoln green. I should do a very good trade with you, for there are at least a hundred of you."

"You seem very sure that we would pay you for your goods!" said Little John.

"So sure," replied the traveller, "that it will not be long before you will see me again."

Robin gave the man a good meal of venison before he went on his way. When the travelling merchant arrived at the villages, he told the people how well Robin had treated him, and the reason why he was spared. Thus the villagers knew that Robin and his Merrie Men were their friends. Robin's own men, too, had been taught a valuable lesson that day—that they were not to harm the interests of the common folk.

The traveller was as good as his word. Not more than a week had gone by when he returned with his horse laden with cloth of Lincoln green. The outlaws paid him in full for his material, and he rode off well content.

Yet only a few days later he was back, and there was trouble written on his face.

"After I left you," he told Robin Hood, "I must have taken the wrong path near Nottingham, for in the dusk I was set upon by a band of robbers. The fiends took all my money and my horse. I was left there to find my own way home."

"Take us to the place where you went astray," said Robin.

Somewhat unwillingly, the man did so.

"I think it was here that I wandered off the right path,"

he said, after they had gone a long distance.

Robin and his Merrie Men searched thoroughly for signs of a struggle, but they could find none. Robin noted this and sent two of his men to visit the traveller's house and his shop in the town. He was suspicious about the truth of the story he had been told, but he gave no sign of this to the traveller.

"I'm afraid you will have to remain with us as our guest," said Robin, "until we can find out who stole your goods."

The man had no option but to stay, and it was not until late the following afternoon that Robin's messengers returned. As they came out of the forest into the camp clearing, Robin, who had been waiting for them, went forward to meet them.

"The man has lied!" they said. "When we visited his stable we found, safely inside, the horse he told us had been stolen."

Robin had suspected as much. He was very angry. He strode over to the traveller.

"You are a fine trader," he said. "You thought to yourself, 'Robin Hood and his Merrie Men have good hearts. I will go and return to them, and tell them I have been robbed, and then perhaps they will give me money to help me.' It was your bad luck that you told me your horse was stolen, for my men found it in your stable."

The man trembled at these angry words.

"I am sorry, good master!" he cried. "Spare me! I will never cheat again!"

He was desperately afraid now that he was found out, that his life would be forfeit.

Robin was silent for a moment. Then he said, "You lied for money, and with money shall you pay your sentence. You will stay here until, at your own request, someone from your home shall bring a ransom. Every penny that you made from us when you sold us the cloth you must hand back. We only want your profits. We would not stoop to rob you of what the cloth actually cost you in the first place."

The wretched cheat had to agree. Robin's terms were carried out. A member of the traveller's family brought to Sherwood Forest the correct amount of money, and the traveller was then allowed to go home.

By this example, the justice that was in the mind of Robin Hood began to dawn on his Merrie Men. They began to understand that it was not Robin's intention to hurt ploughman or labourer. In fact, he had no wish to harm even a high-born knight who was honest and good. But if he knew of anyone cheating, or robbing, or lying, he aimed to mete out to the offender such justice as would be most fitting. If any of the outlaws' captives claimed to have no money, yet when searched were found to possess it, then, because of the lie, they were made to hand over a double gift.

"Help the good folk, and those who find life difficult," said Robin to his band, "but treat those who make it difficult as our enemies—with the Sheriff of Nottingham as the chief!"

5

Robin Hood's Inn

It was near noontide in Sherwood Forest. Overhead the summer sun shone high and hot, piercing the branches and broad leaves of the giant oaks, falling in great splashes of yellow light upon the forest grass, making all the woodlands warm and still. Half the forest-world seemed lulled into a noonday sleep. Only the birds twittered joyously, and the insects kept time to their tuning, humming a drowsy lullaby.

Under the mighty tree, that all Sherwood knew as Robin Hood's Oak, a man in green stood lazily, his back to the huge mossy trunk, staring absently up into the branches over his head. He was tall and fine-limbed, with a much-tanned face, merry brown eyes that twinkled constantly, a head of curling brown hair, and a short beard of the same colour. He stood with one green-clothed leg crossed over its fellow, his green cap was tucked carelessly into his belt. A tall quarter-staff and a great bow and arrows lay on the grass at his feet.

Presently the stillness of the forest-world was broken by the sound of footsteps, firm and hasty, brushing aside the underwood, and next instant three more green-coated men came into sight in the open space before the big oak tree. They came up to the absent faced fellow leaning against the tree trunk, and two of them sank down upon the grass, whilst the third, the tallest of all, stood still and said:

"Dinner awaits ye, Master Robin, at your lodge."

"And 'tis as fine a piece of deer's flesh," added Midge, the miller's son, from the grass, "as ever I turned upon a spit." He rolled over on his back and licked his lips.

"And there is trout fresh from the stream," put in Will Scarlet who sat beside him.

Little John, the tall man, still stood and looked at his leader. Robin slowly turned his eyes from the green branches above him and looked at his companions, smiling; then:

"I have no mind to dine—yet," he said.

Scarlet sat bolt upright with a jerk; "Are ye ailing, master?"

"Nay," the other smiled broader; "but a good dinner is naught without a guest to share it. I lack a guest."

"Do ye say so?" Midge waved a hand towards his companions. "Here are three," he laughed, "and the rest of the lads await ye at the lodge."

"I meant a stranger guest. See here, men. I have a mind that some fine soul shall dine with me today. Therefore, take your ways to the highway—to Watling Street—and bring me the first noble stranger who passes along."

"To share the dinner?" Little John bowed. "But what manner of stranger, say ye?"

"Archbishop or bishop," came the answer, "abbot or haughty knight, or any that has a proud bearing; but the poor folk ye know well, and them shall ye let pass without a word. I will await ye at the lodge."

"Ye shall not wait long," answered Little John with a flourish, and the other two sprang to their feet. All three started off, but Robin called them back for an instant, and then, his eyes twinkling, wagged a warning finger at them.

"Keep in your minds," he said solemnly, "the High Sheriff of Nottingham." At that the others roared with laughter, for the Sheriff, a meddling, blustering, pompous fellow, who had sworn that Robin and his rogues should all be some day caught and clapped in Nottingham Castle and then hung, was their open foe. But they laughed at him, nevertheless, for Master Sheriff had by no means a brave heart, and his "some day" was very long in coming, because it was known that he had a wholesome fear of Robin's army of men in green.

The three friends swung quickly through the forest, and came out at last upon the highway that bordered it upon one side. The long road stretched before them, empty, and hot, and white beneath the glaring sun; and the men took up their stand behind a great beech tree by the water-side and there set themselves to wait.

For a long time they were quite silent. The sunny country-side was very still, and not a single traveller, afoot or on horseback, passed up or down the road beneath the beech tree. Presently Will Scarlet yawned.

"I am hungry," he said in a grumbling tone, and slid to the grass. "I'll warrant they'll not wait for us at the lodge, and meantime we might stay here till sundown before—"

"Sh-h!" It was Little John's voice, coming warningly.

Will Scarlet looked up, craned his neck round the tree-trunk, and then noiselessly got to his feet.

A hundred yards away, upon the dusty road, a man was riding slowly down towards the beech tree. His steed, ambling steadily on, with drooping head and ears, seemed utterly weary and without spirit; the man himself no less so. He had a noble, kindly face, with mournful eyes and a gentle mouth. His tunic, cloak, and cap, once of costly scarlet velvet and silk, were battered, soiled, and weather-stained. As he rode, he stared straight ahead with a sorrowful, vacant gaze that seemed to see nothing. He held the bridle slackly, his head drooped like his horse's, one foot hung limply out of the stirrup, as if the rider had forgotten that he was mounted upon a steed at all.

The three men, hidden behind the tree, watched him curiously for an instant. The tired horse ambled on. "A knight!" whispered Will Scarlet at last. "As I live, a knight, and a noble one! Now—"

They stepped into the road, three tall, fine figures in green. The horse came to a standstill as they blocked his way.

Little John stepped forward, bowing low, feathered cap in hand. Then he laid a firm hand on the bridle.

"You are welcome, Sir Knight," he said in smooth tones, "right welcome to us in the greenwood. My master awaits you to join him at dinner."

"Ah!" The man on the horse straightened himself, and looked at John, as though he were bringing his thoughts back to the present from a long way off. "Yes," he said in a far-away tone; "who may your master be, good fellow?"

John smiled. "Robin Hood is his name, sir," he answered.

Something like a gleam of interest came into the mournful eyes.

"I have heard of him," said the knight gently, and nodded. "I have heard, too, that he is a good yeoman and a gentleman. Well, since it is his will and your will, lead me to him. Though," he added, sighing, "I did purpose to push on to Doncaster town, and there to dine."

"You will fare as well at Robin Hood's Inn in merry Sherwood as at any hostel in Doncaster town," Midge assured him, and turned the tired steed towards the shady forest.

The knight gave a sad little smile, and fell into silence. The three men looked at one another as they led horse and rider deep into the woods, but something made them keep silent, too, and the little procession went on its way slowly.

Again the look in the knight's eyes had grown faraway and sorrowful. Several times he sighed heavily, and once raised his frayed silk sleeve hastily, to brush away some gathering tears.

"Bless me!" whispered Will Scarlet in Midge's ear at last. "Have we ever brought to our Robin such a grieving guest as this Master Melancholy? What, man! We are not leading him to his hanging!" But Little John frowned him into silence, and so, still in silence, they came to the outlaws' woodland lodge.

Robin Hood came out to receive them, merry-eyed and smiling, his bare brown head shining in the sunshine.

"Welcome!" he cried, "Sir Guest! Welcome and thrice welcome to Robin Hood's Inn! We have waited long for you." He helped the knight from his horse, still talking, and something in his cheery tones seemed to arouse the sad-faced stranger.

"I am glad to meet you also, friend," he said, "I have heard very much of Robin Hood, and of his merry men."

The lodge was large and airy, formed of tree-trunks and cut boughs cunningly built and intertwisted to form secure walls and a roof; and, within, Robin brought his guest water in a quaintly carved bowl, that he might wash away the dust of travel. But, because of the heat of the day, the dinner had been laid outside, spread out upon a fine linen cloth upon the soft green grass.

Of food and drink there was plenty, and that all of the best. Wheaten bread and rich wine, white fish from the streams, deer's flesh and fowl and fruit—all these were kindly pressed upon the stranger, for Robin and his men knew how to entertain a guest right royally when they set their minds to the matter. In the face of so much kindliness and good cheer, a little of the knight's sadness seemed to melt away. He put aside his shabby cloak, lay full length in the shade upon the cool grass, and talked and listened, and even smiled. Then Robin, ever proud of his followers' skill, insisted that he show his guest a trial of shooting with bow and arrows after which tall Midge and Little John had a bout with their oaken quarter-staves; and everything the knight watched and praised, and declared that Robin Hood's men were the finest in the country, and he knew of no yeomen to match them. So they passed that long afternoon of summer sunshine; but when the sun, a fiery globe, showed low in the sky through the woodland trees, the stranger rose and said he must be riding.

"And I thank you, master," he turned to Robin, "for the best and pleasantest dinner I have eaten this many a long week. Be assured that, if ever I ride these ways again, you shall not need to call for such a dinner in return, if I can provide it for you." The old sad look crept back again, and once more he sighed.

Robin smiled at the words.

"I should be hungry and greedy both, I think, indeed," he said, "to be driven to call (Saint Hubert preserve me!) upon any man for a dinner. But come," his pleasant tone did not change but grew suddenly firmer, "I must tell ye the custom of Robin Hood's Inn, and the password, which is, 'Pay ere ye wend'. Come, Sir Knight, ye have had dinner—and a good dinner—from a yeoman's hands. But it was never the custom—think ye so?—for a yeoman to pay for a knight." Then he came closer, and the men in green clustered about him. "Pay ere ye wend sir," he said.

A little frown of distress came between the knight's brows; he looked straight into Robin's eyes, then dropped his own, flushing red.

"I am ashamed," he said in a low voice, "that what I have with me—all I have in the world—is not enough to give in payment for so good a dinner to so gentle a host."

"How!" Robin lifted his eyebrows in astonishment, and at the same time his lips made a motion to Little John: "Go and look," he said; and John stepped over and took up the knight's cloak, searching his pockets. "Now," Robin looked full at the man before him, "tell me the truth, as ye claim to be a true knight, sir." And the knight looked back at him, sadly and steadfastly, then answered:

"This is the truth, good master, and so may Heaven help me! I have no more than ten shillings in all this world."

Again the outlaw looked at him, and this time there was gentleness in his brown eyes. "I think ye speak the truth indeed," he said, "and, if it be so, not a penny shall we take from ye, but rather, if ye have need of it, we can lend ye more."

The knight turned aside in silence, his face to the slow-sinking red sun. Little John laid down the cloak and stepped close to his leader.

"Master," he whispered in Robin's ear, "it is even as he says, poor soul. There are but ten shillings there."

The outlaw's eyes grew soft again. He walked over to his guest and touched the sleeve of his shabby tunic very gently.

"Come," he said, "Sir Knight, let us talk over this matter across a bowl of wine. Tell me your name, truly, and, truly also, whether ye be a noble knight and an honourable one, and what evil fortune has led ye to such a pass as this." He flung himself upon the grass as he spoke, and the stranger sat down beside him.

"I tell you no more than the truth, Master Robin," he said, "when I tell you that I am a true knight and an honourable one, as my ancestors have been for a hundred years before me, and my name is Sir Richard Lea." He smiled a little, and then sighed, and went on:

"In my happier days—not so far gone, alas!—I had all that a man might crave for—houses and lands and riches; but Heaven hath seen fit to take all these from me and to leave me naught but my wife and my children. The sweet saints be thanked," he finished half to himself, "I still have them!"

"And how came ye," Robin questioned, "to lose land and money both?"

"I had a son," said the knight in a low voice, "a lad of twenty, who, in a quarrel, slew a noble knight of Lancashire and his squire. It was to save him from shame that I have sold my goods and given my riches."

"And your lands, sir?" questioned Robin again.

"They are forfeit too. I have signed a bond to a rich abbot, whom ye may know, of Saint Mary's Abbey. He will take them all too readily, for alas! as ye see, I have nothing left to redeem them."

"And the money that he pays?"

"Ah! With that I must leave this fair country, and sail away to foreign lands and hide my head beneath an eastern sky."

"Will ye tell me the sum that ye owe?" asked Robin gently.

"Four hundred pounds," was the heavy answer, and again the knight got to his feet. "See, the sun is low behind the trees. I and my poor fortunes must be going. Fare you well, good master, and again thanks."

"Nay, softly, sir." Robin's hand was on his sleeve again. "Where are thy friends?" he said. "Is there not one who would lend thee the sum to redeem those lands that are forfeit?"

The knight gave a little bitter laugh.

"Whilst I had plenty and to spare I had friends, many a one; but now they would tell ye they had no use for a man's empty coffers and cupboard."

The men in green looked at one another, and then looked away. Little John turned aside, muttering: "Now, may the saints bear me witness, that this is the most sorrowful story ever I heard."

"Well, well," Robin scrambled to his feet, smiling, "I think no man fallen upon evil fortunes ever fell so low but that he might fall even lower. Come, I know ye for a true knight, Sir Richard, and I can well lend ye the sum ye stand in need of. Go to my treasury, John, and count out four hundred pounds; and, John, see that ye stint not in the counting."

Like an arrow Little John was off, and Midge and Will Scarlet after him. In the lodge they opened Robin's coffers, so well filled with gold and silver, and there John counted out the sum in scores, but every score was two and twenty pounds in gold pieces.

"Faith!" cried Midge, looking on, "John, methinks that is a new way of counting."

"What would ye?" John demanded, "'tis alms for a poor and gentle knight."

Back at Robin's side with the money-bags, "Master," he said, "the knight's clothes seem neither so warm nor so fine as they once were. He must have a new suit—what say ye? Give him some of your scarlet and green—ye have as goodly a store of cloth as any merchant in fair England."

"By my head, and that is true!" cried Robin. "Measure out for him three yards of every colour of cloth, full measure, mind ye." And from the piles of bright silk and velvet and cloth, John measured off yards that were six feet long instead of three, for he took no measure but his own mighty bow of yew.

"Ye would make but a poor draper," observed Midge, dryly, but Will Scarlet roared with laughter, and said John could afford to give good measure since 'twas costing him nothing in the giving.

When the bundles of cloth and the money bags were securely packed, John spoke again.

"Master, he cannot carry all this on foot. He must have another horse."

"Saddle the new grey courser, then," smiled Robin, "and see that the saddle be a new one."

"Nay, give him a horse to ride, and a palfrey to carry the goods," chuckled Midge. "And a pair of boots, master," put in Will Scarlet.

"And thou, Little John"—Robin turned to his favourite—"what wouldst thou give him?"

"A pair of gilt spurs," answered John very heartily, "and the wish that Heaven may speedily help him to better fortunes."

They pressed around Sir Richard, offering this and that. One held his horse as he mounted, a second tied his bales and bags upon a sturdy little palfrey, a third fastened the glittering spurs to the shining new boots. Half bewildered, the knight spoke to Robin:

"When shall the day of payment be, master, to return in full so many kindnesses?"

"Why, this day twelvemonth," came the careless answer, "here under this greenwood tree."

"I will remember," said Sir Richard solemnly; but Robin looked at him thoughtfully for an instant, then at Little John, and then back again at the knight.

"Ye should have a squire or yeoman to attend ye," he said. "Here, sir—I will lend ye Little John for as long as ye need him, for he will serve ye well and faithfully; and when ye want him no longer he shall come back to me. And now farewell, and Heaven be with you, sir."

The men in green drew up in a body, and watched the knight and his new follower set off slowly, through the dusky woods, upon their journey, following the little procession with their eyes until it was lost between the trees.

Then Will Scarlet gave a little laugh.

"Think you he will come back upon the day of reckoning, master?" he said.

"Aye," Robin answered quietly, "I think he will."

And he was right, for when the year rolled round once more, and summer came again to the greenwood, it brought with it the faithful Little John, and the no less faithful Sir Richard Lea, laden with wealth enough to pay off his debt in full to the kindly hosts at Robin Hood's Inn.

6

Robin and the Bishop

"It is over long, friends," sighed Robin, "since an adventure came our way."

He sat with his back against his favourite oak tree, screened by its thickly-clustering leaves and branches from the morning sunshine, carefully fitting, one by one, new arrow-heads upon a bundle of long arrows at his side.

The men in green, as usual, were all about him. Little John, on a fallen tree-trunk, fitted a new string to his great bow, whistling softly over the task. Midge, the miller's son, lay full length upon a bank of moss, idly throwing acorn-cups at a too curious squirrel in a beech tree ten yards away. At his master's words he sat up and yawned.

"Ye speak truth, indeed," he said. "'Tis time something happened. But I think the heat and the sunshine have put all the world to sleep, or else all the world is enchanted, for the doings of every day are mighty dull, and if we want adventure—why, it cometh not, even for the seeking, and we—"

A whoop from a distant glade startled them all, and next instant a band of green coated fellows, headed by Will Scarlet, dashed up to the great oak.

"Oh, news, master!" panted out that shock-headed

fellow, "news, news, and an adventure!" Robin threw down his arrows, Little John leaped to his feet.

"What?"

"Fine news," repeated Will Scarlet. He took off his green cap and fanned himself, then burst into a laugh, looking at Robin. "What think ye?" he cried then, "a fine company, a rich company, rides through merry Barnsdale today, and at the head of that company rides—who, think ye? Why, none other than my lord the fine, rich, Bishop of Hereford!"

A shout of laughter arose from his listeners. Robin clapped his hands, and patted his follower on the shoulder.

"The best of news!" he laughed, "a rich bishop makes a good guest, and the taking of him shall serve for a merry adventure. Now, hear my plan." He sat down again, his brown eyes twinkling with mischief. The men in green gathered round eagerly.

"First," he went on, "we must kill a fat and lusty deer. Why? For the dinner, to be sure, Midge. And then we will cut and dress it by the side of the highway, and so keep a look out, that our guest, the Bishop, may not miss us, nor ride some other way."

"He will pass by at noon," nodded Will Scarlet.

"The better for us. John, man, take thy bow, and bring me as fine a buck as makes its home in the greenwood. And six of ye, I care not which, make ready to come with me. Meet us in Barnsdale, good John."

Little John slipped swiftly away into the greenwood at once, and Robin and his six men made for the forest lodge. There they stripped off their green suits, and donned, each man, a shepherd's dress of rough skin.

Then, bareheaded and barelegged, seven shaggy rustic figures carrying staves, they set out for the public high road that wound through the great woods.

Little John was there before them, waiting patiently, a fine, freshly-killed deer slung across his big shoulders, but at a word of praise and a whispered order from Robin he lowered it to the grass by the way-side, and vanished once more into the forest.

Then the seven make-believe shepherds set to work, and, whilst one gathered sticks and lit a fire, the others began to cut up and dress the deer skilfully, as only such forest men knew how. It was ten minutes to noon.

"If your Lord Bishop hath gone some other way, master?" chuckled Midge; but at that moment the sound of hoofs on the high road made them all look up, and, as he looked, Robin laughed softly.

"There is no fear of that, Midge," he said. A dozen horses were bearing down towards them, each with his rider, and at their head trotted a big grey mule, splendid with scarlet trappings and a blue-and-gold saddle-cloth. On the mule's back rode my lord the Bishop of Hereford, a small, pink, fat man, puffing noisily in his heavy cloak of purple silk. Those on the horses behind him were a few of his servants.

The cavalcade trotted up the road beneath the trees, now in sunshine, now in shade, a brilliant, many-coloured procession. But my Lord Bishop's sharp little eyes had caught sight of the forest fire and the rough-coated group by the dead deer, and he tugged hard at the grey mule's bridle.

"Hey! Hey! What is this? What have we here?"

His voice was deep and wheezy, and seemed to come

from a long way off. The seven shepherds round the fire turned and faced him, open-mouthed and simple-faced, but made no answer.

"Hey!" cried the Bishop again in a louder tone. "What are you doing here? Fellows, did you kill that deer?"

Robin stepped forward, a big, shaggy figure in his sheepskin.

"Yes, your honour, so please your grace," he said in the country fashion, and the men behind him looked down and laughed noiselessly.

"What!" spluttered the Bishop, taken aback. "You say you killed it, Impudence? Know you not that every deer in Sherwood Forest and in Barnsdale belongs to His Majesty the King?"

"Aye, your lordship," answered Robin again, "but we be a few poor shepherds who spend all the long year a-keeping our sheep, and today we had a mind to be merry, and so—"

He gave a grin, and pointed a brown finger at the deer. The Bishop's fat face went into puckers, and he pursed up his mouth importantly.

"Ah! Well, since ye are such fine fellows, and have, as ye say, a mind to be merry, ye shall come along with me, and tell of your doings to His Majesty."

He blew a silver whistle, and half a dozen of the servants behind him flung themselves down from their horses and advanced towards the men in sheepskin. But Robin ran forward into the road to kneel in the dust before the grey mule, clutching at his lordship's silken cloak.

"Pardon," he snivelled; "oh, pardon, your honour! Would ye take us to be hanged? Alas! Alas! So many of us to die!" He grovelled at the mule's feet, sniffing dismally, and his companions groaned in sympathy.

The Bishop thrust a fine leather-shod foot from his stirrup and pushed the kneeling man backwards.

"Let go of my cloak, fellow!" he blustered. "What! A clown such as you asks for pardon! A knave! A thief caught in the act—in the act, I say! You shall be swung up; aye, every mother's son. Pardon, forsooth!"

His servants gathered close, and some laid hands upon the men in sheepskin. But next instant the mock shepherd was upon his feet, and, swift as lightning, had dragged from beneath his coat a great silver-mounted bugle-horn decked with green ribbons, that flashed before my Lord Bishop's startled eyes.

Robin stepped back, straight and tall, set the horn to his lips, and blew three long echoing blasts.

"Come hither! Come hither! Come hither!" that big horn seemed to cry, and the notes rang, clear and loud, through that still summer-world and over the greenwoods.

A minute's silence fell over the group upon the high road. The Bishop's fat jaw dropped in sheer bewilderment, and in amazement also his servants stood staring. Then a sudden rustling and stirring sound began to grow amongst the forest-trees, and next instant a crowd of green-coated men were pouring fast and thick from the shade of the woodlands into the public way. Faster and faster they flocked in from all sides, that army in green, bearing their great bows; and the Bishop, watching open-mouthed, saw that every man of the company, as he came, bowed low to the man in sheepskin still holding his bugle.

The crowd had closed in upon my Lord Bishop's small band, and then from out of the throng a mighty black-haired man stepped, carrying his giant bow. Then, striding up to the shepherd:

"Lo, we have come at your call, Robin Hood," he cried. "What is your will with us?"

"Here's a grave business, John," Robin answered, but his bright eyes twinkled with fun. "Here is his lordship, the great Bishop of Hereford, and his company, and here are we in sorry plight, their prisoners for stealing the King's deer. We are to have no pardon, and we are to be hanged. Now, what do ye say?"

"Say!" cried Little John. "What do we say? What do we ever say to folk such as these? There's but one word that's worth the saying—kill!"

He laughed grimly, and made a sign to the outlaws, who clustered closer, and whilst a dozen seized upon the Bishop's servants and held them fast, John himself, with a movement of one strong arm, had swept their master, now thoroughly scared, from his seat upon the mule, and dumped him into the dust, and so stood over him, a grim figure, towering and severe. At the sight of his lordship grovelling in the road, his fat face pale with terror, Robin shook with silent laughter, and his companions grinned behind their hands. But it was the trembling Bishop's turn to kneel now, and he caught at Robin's sleeve, turning beseeching eyes upon John

"Oh, pardon, sirs!" he wheezed. "Save me; spare me! Do anything but kill me—Oh, Master Robin Hood, have mercy, have mercy for Saint Charitie's sake! Alas! Had I known who ye were I would not have troubled ye. Indeed, indeed, I would have passed some other way!"

A titter passed through the throng of outlaws, and: "I'll warrant ye would, master!" chuckled Scathelock in the background.

Robin's eyes began to twinkle again and his mouth twitched, but he drew himself up, and said in the Bishop's own pompous voice:

"Let go of my sleeve, fellow! What! A craven such as you asks for pardon! A knave! A Paul-Pry caught in the act—in the act, I say! Pardon, forsooth! Ye shall come along with me!"

He mimicked the Bishop's wheezy tones and the Bishop's high manner, whilst a roar of laughter went up from his men, and Midge rolled over helpless on the grass. Then Robin grasped the kneeling man firmly by the shoulder and pulled him to his feet. "Come!" he said again, and so, whilst two of his men took charge of the mule, and the rest drove the Bishop's servants forward in a body, Robin, still holding on to his frightened captive, led the way into the forest.

Dinner had been eaten at the woodland lodge—a plentiful dinner, such as Robin Hood gave to every guest who dined with him—and his lordship the Bishop began to feel a little more at ease. Robin, smiling, and freshly clothed in his suit of Lincoln green, proved himself to be a most courteous host, and pressed his guest to take the best of food and wine. Those fearful-looking bows and arrows were laid out of sight, and thus his lordship calmed his fears, and tried to make the best of an awkward business.

But when the meal had come to an end, the Bishop rose to his feet, muttering an excuse, with one eye on Robin and the other on his men, and said he supposed the outlaws would want payment for so nobly entertaining strangers. Robin stood up too, leaned both hands upon the table, looked in his lordship's face, and laughed softly. "Payment!" he cried. "Why, sir, what else? 'Pay ere ye wend' has ever been the motto at Robin Hood's Inn, and no rich man leaves Sherwood without hearing it, and if he understandeth it not" he played with his sword meaningly.

"Then," mumbled the Bishop hastily, "ye had better call in the—the reckoning, master."

"With the best will in the world." Little John skipped over to my lord's purple cloak, spread it upon the ground, searched every pocket, and finally came back with a large and heavy purse, which he handed to Robin, bowing low.

The outlaw took it, poured out a stream of golden coins upon the table, and counted them. There were three hundred pounds in all. Then, smiling, he handed the empty purse back to the Bishop.

His lordship's greedy eyes almost started from his head, and: "So much?" he gasped.

"So much, indeed," chuckled Little John, "and i' faith, Bishop, 'tis so much and such a goodly sum that it almost makes me—love thee." Then, as his companions shouted, "Though I know," he added sweetly, "that thou lovest not me in return."

"Aye, so much." Robin echoed the Bishop's words, half-smiling, half-grave. He came close and tapped the other's fat shoulder.

"Know that it is ever Robin Hood's way, my lord, to take from the rich and give to the poor. Your purse has been too heavy this many a day. See to it in future that the poor may lighten it of its burden, and ye shall be a happier man."

His brown eyes sought the Bishop's sternly as he spoke, then lit up with laughter again, and his voice changed.

"But come!" he cried. "A preaching is but a sorry ending to a feast! Come, come, music and a dance!"

He stepped back, and gave a signal, whereupon Will Scarlet, leaning against a tree, began to play a lively tune upon his pipe. The notes poured out, quick and merry, and Robin, beating an impatient foot upon the grass, cried, "Come!" once more. But the Bishop stared, blinking stupidly, until Little John strode over and gave him a light shake. "Dance!" he commanded shortly, and his companions seized each of his lordship's servants, and set them on their feet.

"Dance!" cried the outlaws together, and drew their swords, whilst Will Scarlet went on playing.

And so my Lord Bishop of Hereford and his men were forced to dance, although sadly against their will and in spite of their dignity.

Faster and faster came Will Scarlet's tune, faster and faster the Bishop was made to jig and prance and skip—a fat, foolish figure in his purple cloak, panting and blowing, his face almost the colour of his cloak, the moisture rolling down his puckered forehead. But dance on he must, for the outlaws had closed round, a bristling ring of greencoats, and at each new step they broke into fresh roars of laughter called forth by his lordship's capers.

For the rest of that hot summer's afternoon, with scarce time for breathing, the Bishop danced to Will

Scarlet's playing, nor dared he and his servants stop until the outlaws, holding their aching sides, declared they could laugh no more, and Robin called a halt.

And when the sun slipped, red and low, behind the tree-trunks, it was a very humbled and spiritless Bishop who slunk at last out of Sherwood Forest at the rear of his weary company. But he kept ever in mind his visit to Robin, and passed no more through Barnsdale; nor did he ever again meddle with the doings of the men in green.

7

The Defenders of Gamwell Hall

Robin longed to see Maid Marian once again. He knew that she was staying at Gamwell Hall now, as the guest of Squire Gamwell. Word had come to Robin that a party of the Sheriff's men had come to the Hall and charged Squire Gamwell with having shot one of the King's deer.

There had been a great battle between the Sheriff's men and the servants of Squire Gamwell. The guests that were staying at the Hall also joined in. Amongst them was Maid Marian's father.

At the height of the battle, Marian's father went to an open window and shot at the Sheriff's men. He killed many of the men with his fine shooting, but he was at last shot himself. He was taken into an inner room, and, a little later, he died.

Squire Gamwell felt very sorry for the little Maid Marian, and he told her that she could stay at Gamwell Hall with him for as long as she wished.

So Robin set out with Little John for Gamwell Hall, to see once more his childhood friend. Squire Gamwell was delighted to see Robin again. Robin introduced Little John to the Squire, and the two became friends at once. Robin's cousin, Will Gamwell, was glad that his old friend had returned. They talked for a long time.

Robin told Will all that had happened since they had last met, and he added that if ever Will wanted to join his band he could offer him a life of freedom and excitement.

Robin, Will Gamwell, and Little John were walking through the Hall with Maid Marian, laughing and joking about old times, when Squire Gamwell burst in upon them with a very worried face.

"We are surrounded!" he said. "The Sheriff's men must have found out about your coming here."

Robin rushed at once to the window and peered into the forest, beyond the grounds of the Hall. He saw the Sheriff's men hiding in the undergrowth. There were many of them; they were well armed, and it was clear that they were in deadly earnest.

"This may be the end of everything!" said Squire Gamwell.

Robin and Little John laughed.

"It's just the sort of thing that makes life worth living," said Little John.

A tall, broad-shouldered member of the Sheriff's company bent his bow and shot an arrow towards the Hall.

"The fight has begun!" said Robin.

It was now getting dark, and little could be gained by either side. Robin knew that the next day would bring with it the full force of the battle. He knew, also, that he could take advantage of the blackness of the night to defeat the Sheriff.

He quickly worked out a plan that could be put into force at once.

"We'll show them that we are not afraid," he cried.

"Who will swim the moat with me and surprise these varlets?"

Robin never asked anyone to do what he himself would not do.

Little John quickly joined him.

In those days all the largest halls had moats around them as a protection against attack from enemies. The Sheriff's men had drawn themselves together in the forest as night fell, feeling sure that nothing would happen until the light of day.

Will Gamwell followed Little John and joined Robin. Finally, two of Squire Gamwell's servants also volunteered to help.

It was an easy matter for Robin and his four friends to swim the moat and to clamber on to the bank without being seen.

As they reached the encampment where the Sheriff's men were resting, Robin very quickly told the others what he meant to do. It needed brave men to pounce upon those sleeping soldiers, for, once awakened, there would be little chance of escape for the attackers. But Robin stepped fearlessly forward. With the other men close behind him, he charged into the sleeping men, and swords flashed left and right.

The Sheriff's men were soon awake. They sprang up at once. They could not understand what was happening, for it was quite dark, and there was a scene of complete confusion. In the blackness of the night, the Sheriff's men attacked each other, not knowing who was who. Everyone was fighting with whatever weapon he could lay his hands on, and in the melee that followed Robin and his four gallant friends withdrew and made again for the moat.

Four of them were able to escape into the water and to swim safely to the Hall. But the fifth, one of the servants who had volunteered to join Robin, was slower than the rest, and he was caught by two of the Sheriff's men.

Robin at once started to go back to the rescue of the servant, but Squire Gamwell, when he knew what had happened, would not hear of it. He wanted the servant rescued, but it was very doubtful whether the Sheriff's men would do anything with their captive until daylight.

"Wait till morning," he said.

Robin arranged that all the men should take it in turns to keep watch from the Hall all through the night, so that any move on the part of the Sheriff and his men could be spotted. Then he ordered all the other members who were not acting as sentries to go to sleep. He wanted them to be fresh for the battle on the following day.

Maid Marian was the first to rise. She called the others as soon as day broke.

"Come!" she called to Robin. "See from this window what the men are doing with our servant."

Robin sprang to the window, and saw that the servant was about to be hanged by the Sheriff's men.

There was no time to be lost. He ordered the defenders of the Hall to finish the meal that they were eating and make ready for an attack.

He went to the window again. One of the men had climbed a tree. He carried over his shoulder a length of rope. This he tied to a bough of the tree. Underneath the bough stood a second man with the servant, who was awaiting his end without fear.

Robin called to Will Gamwell.

"Shoot the man in the tree!" he said. "And, whatever happens, do not miss!"

Will Gamwell aimed his bow carefully. Just as the arrow was winged to the target, Robin shot at the man on the ground. Both of the Sheriff's men fell. The man in the tree came tumbling through the branches and lay still on the ground.

The servant was now free, and he lost no time in running towards the moat. In he plunged and swam desperately for the Hall. Friendly hands pulled him safely out of the water when he reached the other side.

The Sheriff's men had had enough. They knew that only a long siege would now make Robin and the defenders of Gamwell Hall give in. So they withdrew, for they had not come prepared for a prolonged conflict.

They returned to the Sheriff's castle and told him what had taken place. He was furious when he learned of their failure.

8

The Tale of Friar Tuck

"There is no life like that of the greenwood," sighed Robin contentedly, one evening, as he and his followers clustered round their forest-fire in the gloaming, after a long day's hunting.

He looked round at the merry men as he spoke, and smiled happily. "No life like the greenwood life," he repeated; "and surely there are not in the world any fitter companions to share such a life than you—friends and comrades. I'll wager that within a hundred miles of Sherwood there is no man who's a match for any of us, more skilled with sword and quarter-staff, or handier with his bow."

"There's none, certainly, who can match you, master," cried Will Scarlet proudly.

"But there is the Friar of Fountains Abbey," put in a voice above their heads.

It was Midge, the miller's son, who spoke. He had perched himself high up on the overhanging bough of a big oak tree, and he sat there at ease, swinging his legs and munching an apple.

"And who may the Friar of Fountains Abbey be?" demanded Robin.

Midge took another bite from his apple, and then began to explain with his mouth full.

"He lives a matter of a few score miles from Sherwood here, they say, like a hermit in a cell. A monk he is, and, so I have heard, a pious and godly one; but I have heard also that he has met no man yet who is his master either in fighting, or in the use of bow and arrow."

"I would like to see him!" exclaimed Robin eagerly, with shining eyes.

"Oh, well," Midge laughed, and swayed gently up and down on his bough, "pay him a visit, pay him a visit, master. He welcomes all comers. Faith! I'd well like to see the meeting between ye. And I'd like also," he muttered to himself, eyeing his leader with pride, "to see the fellow who'll be a match for our Robin."

But Robin, eager for any adventure, and fired by Midge's description of the curious friar, took his follower at his word; and, early next morning, set off alone through the woods to seek for the monk.

All that day he tramped northwards, and, when night fell, slept soundly under a tree until the sunshine awoke him once more. Then again he set forth on his journey, going easily, determined to discover the object of his search, yet heedless of the time he spent upon finding it.

Early on the morning of the third day he crossed a long, green hill, entered a straggling wood that lay at the foot of it, and presently, turning aside from the uneven path, found himself beside a stream—a clear, quick-flowing rill, bordered by clumps of bracken and patches of wild forget-me-not.

As he followed the water it widened, and Robin, looking ahead, saw that it ran in the sunlight through a broad clearing between the trees. At the farther end of this open glade was a huge rock, almost a cliff, crowned with waving rowan trees, and tufted here and there among its stones with clusters of wild fern. In the face of the rock was an arched opening, hollowed like the entrance of a cave. A few rocky steps led up to it, a small bell hung over the open doorway, and before the entrance sat a man.

He was perched upon a low stool, set on the flowery grass near the water's edge. His head was shaven his feet were bare, his face was calm, but full of humour. He wore a monk's long robe of brown, with a brown cowl, and he was bending eagerly over a book that rested on his knee.

All these things Robin's quick eye noted, but he noted also, what to him was the strangest thing of all, that the friar (for such he certainly was) wore a long, bright sword at his side, slung at his hip by a fanciful belt, and that on the grass beside him lay a round steel buckler or shield.

"Is this the Friar of Fountains Abbey?" muttered Robin to himself, "Now, if he prove so, then this is the strangest man of peace that ever I beheld in all my life. Hath he a tongue in his head, I wonder?"

He stepped out in the sunlight, and moved over the grass towards the monk.

"Good morrow to you, father!" he said in a soft tone.

The friar lifted his head from his book, and looked the newcomer over calmly. He seemed in no way surprised at this stranger's appearance, neither did he show any sign of fear at the big man in green who stood over him, bearing his great bow and his sheaf of bristling arrows. His bright blue eyes met Robin's shrewd and merry brown ones, and, as they did so, he broke into a slow smile.

"Good morrow to you also, friend!" he said civilly.

There was silence for a moment. A mischievous plan was forming in Robin's freakish head. He came close up to the friar.

"I wish to cross the stream," he said simply, "and the water is wide here, and flows deeply, and belike I should stumble, for I do not know the ford. Will you please to bear me across, father, upon your shoulders?"

The other looked him up and down again; Robin's eyes were looking straight into his, with not a glint of mischief in them, and, besides, the request was made quite courteously; it would have been churlish to refuse.

"Yes, I will," he said, and put down his book, standing up. Then he took the tall man in green upon his shoulders, clasped him firmly, gathered up his robe, and stepped into the cool water.

He evidently knew the ford well, for he waded through swiftly and without stumbling, and presently he and his burden were safely landed on the opposite bank, and Robin slid to the ground with a "Thank you, father."

But the monk came close up to him, and as he did so, drew his sword from its scabbard.

"Behold, master," he said in his deep voice, "I have borne ye across the stream, and now I am myself upon the wrong side of it, for yonder bank is the place where I choose to sit, and there I was when ye first came upon me. Will you please to bear me back, then, upon your shoulders?" He mimicked Robin's simple tone, and flashed his long sword significantly before the other's eyes.

Robin looked at him an instant, and his lips twitched. Then:—

"Well, father, that is but fair," he said, and hoisted the friar upon his own broad back. But as he stepped into the water, he brought one hand craftily round to the side where his companion's sword hung, and pulled the belt loose, very gently, so that, when the two were in mid-stream, sword and scabbard and belt fell with a splash into the water. The friar cried out in annoyance, but Robin took no heed, and waded on, until he had reached the bank and dumped the other down upon his seat again.

"Now," he cried, "let us have no more fooling, friar. I wish to get to the other side, and you must carry me. Come!"

The monk bit his lip, flushing. His sword was gone, and he was all at the other's mercy. He made a wry face, but replied: "Well, since ye will have it so," and, lifting the outlaw up again, stepped for the second time into the stream. But if he chose to walk firmly at first, he did not this time, for half-way across he purposely missed his footing, jogged, stumbled, and came near to falling headlong; whilst Robin, losing his balance completely, was hurled violently from his shoulders, and fell head over heels into the water.

Snorting angrily, the outlaw waded to the bank, a big, sorry figure, with all his green finery bedraggled and dripping. Once more upon firm ground, he shook himself like an angry dog, then raised his clenched fist at the friar.

"Ah! Scurvy fellow!" he spluttered.

The monk watched him calmly, standing barefooted in mid-stream, his long robe lifted a little from the water. At the other's outburst his little eyes shone. "I slipped upon my sword," he announced gravely. Then he bent down and groped in the clear water at his feet, where, after a moment's searching, he found his sword, and bore it across to the other bank, where, sitting down, he coolly began to wipe his dripping weapon upon his robe.

Robin's quick temper was now thoroughly aroused. He was many miles from Sherwood, the day was wearing late, he was hungry also, and now most uncomfortably wet. And, worst of all, he had been outwitted, and that by a monk—a barefooted fellow with a shaven crown—the Friar of Fountains Abbey. Moreover, the sight of that very friar, sitting dry and smiling and at ease upon the farther bank, was enough, Robin considered, to fill any man with rage.

Setting his teeth hard, he went swiftly upon one knee on the grass, fitted an arrow to his bow, and next instant had sent it whistling across within an inch of the friar's right ear. But the latter merely smiled a little broader, put down his sword leisurely, and caught up his buckler, which he held in front of him with so much skill that the now fast-showering rain of the outlaw's arrows did him no harm at all.

At length Robin flung down his bow, weary of this one-sided combat, and plucked at his sword, splashing through the stream to the opposite bank as he did so.

"Come and show how ye can use that blade of

yours!" he cried, and at that the friar, still smiling, cast his buckler to the grass, and caught up his own weapon, at the same time rolling up his long sleeves.

"With all my heart!" he said pleasantly; then added with a soft laugh: "My sword is quite dry now!"

Robin snorted again, and fell upon him furiously, but it did not take him long to discover that in the Friar of Fountains Abbey he had met his match. Monk as he was, he was also a fighting man, and again and again as Robin tried to get the advantage, again and again did he fail. The outlaw's blood was up, and he cut and thrust savagely; the friar was nimble and clever, and meant to show what he was made of; so the fight went on.

The warm June afternoon began to grow cool, the depths of the woodlands became shadowy, and the sun slipped down, a red ball, out of sight behind the trees. Still the two men fought on, with no advantage to either side; only at times, as by a common agreement, they drew apart for a space of rest, eyeing each other and panting; then, after a few seconds had passed, they closed together again.

But the long fighting had dried Robin's clothes and cooled his wrath, and, moreover, an odd liking was springing up at the back of his mind for this sturdy Friar of Fountains Abbey.

The red sun vanished altogether behind the trees, leaving a faint, rosy flush behind it; and again, through sheer weariness, the two men fell apart. Then Robin broke into great laugh—a long jovial laugh that echoed through that silent glade—a laugh in which the friar joined heartily as he watched him.

"Oh," cried the outlaw at last when he could speak,

"are we not two crazy-heads, Sir Friar? To fight for well-nigh half of a sweet summer's day, and—what at the end of it? Where's our quarrel, and what have we fought about?"

"Saints! I have clean forgotten!" laughed the other, and put up his sword, chuckling, whilst Robin slid his own weapon back into its sheath, then crossed the grass and took the other by the arm.

"Let us sit awhile and rest," he said happily. "My name is Robin Hood. Did ye guess that?"

"As soon as I set eyes on ye."

"And your name?"

"Men call me the Friar of Fountains Abbey," smiled the blue-eyed monk whimsically, "but I call myself Friar Tuck."

"And ye live here?"

"In yonder cell." He jerked his head towards the rocky cave. "I have no mind for the cloisters, but I love a free life and the merry greenwood."

Robin jumped to his feet.

"Then come home with me," he cried, "come back to Sherwood with me, and my merry men will welcome us both; and there ye shall live the life ye love, and be our chaplain—our Friar Tuck. Is it a bargain?"

The friar's face had lightened up at the words.

"A bargain indeed!" he cried, "and one that I think neither side will regret in the days to come. I will serve you, Robin Hood, with all my heart."

And, as they turned their faces towards Sherwood in the gloaming, a star shone out and lighted them upon their homeward way.

9

The Tale of Alan-a-Dale

"Let us take a walk through the forest," suggested Robin one quiet summer evening.

"You have more energy than six men put together," laughed Maid Marian, as she finished the last patch on one of the outlaw's suits.

Together they set out through the greenwood, drinking in the sounds and scents of the forest, which shone green and gold in the evening sunlight.

"It's good to be alive on an evening like this," said Maid Marian, happily.

"Hark!" cried Robin suddenly. "It sounds as if someone in the forest agrees with you."

From a short distance ahead came the musical sound of a well-trained baritone voice, singing a tuneful ballad of the day. There seemed to be a hush over the woodland while the voice sang out, as if the animals and birds were listening enraptured.

Robin and Marian walked in the direction of the merry notes. They crossed the border of beech trees that formed the line of a clearing in the forest. Walking cheerfully along on the other side of the open space was a young man. He had a stick in his hand, which at every pause in his song he swished merrily through the air.

Robin pulled Marian back behind a tree as the young man half turned, but he had not seen them, and he walked carelessly onwards, to vanish a moment later into the belt of trees.

"There is a happy young man for you," cried Robin, "one without a care in the world!"

They wandered off in a different direction and took a roundabout route back to the camp.

A week later the two were walking again in the same direction when they saw once more the merry youth whose song had rung through the forest. Now, however, he was lying full length in the grass, silent and sad. Only his bright orange hose betrayed him to Robin and Marian as they wandered into the clearing.

"Perhaps he knows no more songs," whispered Robin, glancing at him.

"There's something strangely sorrowful about him," replied Maid Marian.

Robin and Marian walked towards the youth. At the sound of their footsteps he sprang up, eyeing them with suspicion.

"What do you want?" he demanded.

"We want nothing," returned Robin, "but you looked so dejected lying there that we wished to know if anything ailed you. Only a week ago we saw you here, singing heartily, as if you hadn't a care at all. Yet today it would seem that all the trouble in the world has fallen upon your shoulders."

"If you want to know," said the youth, none too politely, "there is woe enough in my heart."

"Can we help you?"

"No, there is no one who can help me." Then, as if

repenting of his manner, he went on, "A week ago I was going to marry a very beautiful maiden. Ellen is her name. We were planning to be married soon. The world was indeed a good and happy place. Then, this morning, came the dreadful news that tomorrow Ellen must marry a Norman baron."

"And is the Lady Ellen in love with this Norman baron?" asked Maid Marian, in her practical and concerned way.

"Madam she is as heartbroken as I."

"I don't understand," put in Robin. "Tell us more of this, young man. First, what is your name?"

"Men call me Alan-a-Dale," answered the youth.

"And why is the Lady Ellen going to marry the baron?"

"Her father has fallen on hard times," explained Alan-a-Dale. "The Norman baron is rich, and he has offered a large sum of money if Ellen's father will give him his daughter's hand."

"And so poor Ellen will be married to this baron just because the father is in need of money!" exclaimed Maid Marian. "It is a shameful bargain!"

"Where is the wedding to take place?" asked Robin.

"At an abbey near Nottingham."

"Robin," pleaded Maid Marian, "we must help this young man. We can't let two young people in love be parted to please the whim of an autocratic Norman. We must act."

"We will," said Robin. With a determined air, he turned again to Alan-a-Dale. "Have no fear," he said. "The wedding shall be stopped tomorrow. But there is a price. The price shall be that you join my band of outlaws, if Ellen is willing. She would be very good company for Marian."

"I guessed you were Robin Hood," said the young man. "I give you my oath on your demand, for I would have joined you anyway if the marriage had taken place between Ellen and the baron."

"Then come back to my camp with me," Robin invited him. "I will introduce you to my good comrades."

The three walked back to Robin's camp. Robin gathered his men about him, and when they were all seated told them the story of Alan-a-Dale and his lady-love. The outlaws were keen to know how their leader planned to stop the wedding on the following day, but Robin had not then worked out a plan. Later, he sat apart from his band, and thought deeply through the evening.

Early the next morning the Abbey bells pealed out loudly, announcing the wedding to all the townsfolk. Later, inside the Abbey, all the seats were full. Such a large congregation had never before been seen in the old building. Few guessed, however, that it wasn't so much the townspeople's desire to see the marriage as the fact that Robin Hood's men were there in force, disguised as ordinary folk, that swelled the congregation to such an extent.

"Here she comes, now!" the whisper ran round the crowd.

All eyes were turned to the doorway as Ellen, beautiful in her white wedding gown, entered. She was sad at heart and found it hard to smile. She knew her life was being sacrificed to the Norman baron's gold.

A rough, dirty-looking individual thrust himself towards her and her father, who was accompanying her down the aisle.

"I come to bring the maiden luck," laughed the rough-looking fellow.

It was often considered lucky for a tramp or a chimney sweep to be present at a wedding. The three walked up to the altar, where the baron was waiting. His thin lips tightened as he saw the rough vagabond. Impertinent fellow! How dare he accost his future bride? The three figures reached his side. This was not the place to make a scene. The baron remained silent, and beamed at his bride-to-be.

Suddenly he cried out, "Take your hand from me!"

The beam had died on the baron's face, and he shouted loudly as the tramp grabbed him by the scruff of his neck.

"Stand aside," ordered the vagabond, roughly, throwing off his clothes and revealing a suit of Lincoln green.

It was Robin Hood!

Robin faced his men in the congregation and beckoned them to him. They ran to him from all parts of the Abbey.

To the amazement of the Bishop, who was standing ready to perform the ceremony, Robin raised his horn to his lips. Immediately, six archers appeared at the doorway, each with his bow at the ready.

They made way for the entrance of a lone figure. He marched lightly down the aisle. It was Alan-a-Dale. As Ellen recognised him, she gave a cry of delight.

"My Lord Bishop," said Robin, loudly, so that everyone in the Abbey could hear, "you were about to marry two people who would never have been happy.

The bride shall marry the person she loves. Ask her who that is!"

"This is most irregular—" began the outraged Bishop.

"Ask her!" repeated Robin.

"Well, who is it?" asked the Bishop, nervously turning to Ellen.

"Alan-a-Dale is the man I love," replied Ellen, without hesitation.

"Then I cannot perform the ceremony," blustered the Bishop. "I have never been so—"

"That is all right," cut in Robin. "Forward, men!"

Robin's men pushed the infuriated Bishop aside. He struggled to free himself, and two of the outlaws sat on him to keen him quiet.

"The good Friar Tuck shall perform the ceremony," said Robin.

The fat friar ambled down the aisle, with a benign smile on his face. He smiled at Robin, smiled at the Bishop, who was red in the face at the indignity of being sat on, and turned to the lovers standing before him.

Alan-a-Dale and Ellen were married at once. They embraced each other in happy contentment as they became man and wife. What had looked like being a great tragedy ended happily, after all.

10

How Robin Sold Pots at Nottingham Fair

Peter the potter was driving his clumsy little wagon of wares upon a long country road, in the early sunshine of a fresh summer morning.

It was not yet six o'clock. Overhead the larks sang joyously; and in front of him the road wound, curving and white, for half a mile, until it vanished into a mighty patch of dark green forest that lay directly ahead.

The forest was Sherwood Forest, where dwelt that famous outlaw called Robin Hood, with all his merry men. Peter the potter knew that quite well, and many were the tales, mad or merry, that he had heard of this fellow Robin round the cottage fires on winter nights. To a more timid man than the potter it might have seemed a dangerous thing to travel through Sherwood alone and unarmed, even though his pockets were empty. But Peter was a sturdy fellow, and, if he remembered Robin Hood at all this morning, it was merely to wonder what manner of man this outlaw was, and whether he should be likely to meet him upon his way. He had no fear of Sherwood, or Sherwood's merry men.

On he trundled with his little hand-wagon, filled to

the top with earthenware jars, jugs, pots, pans, and basins; and, as he tramped on, pushing it before him, he sang a country ditty in a deep, joyous voice.

Soon the sunny road was left behind him, and he entered the shady woods. How pleasant it was under the trees, with all the sweet forest scents, and the concert of the birds to keep tune to his own singing! But presently he had forgotten his song, and the forest, and the bird-voices all about him, for he was busily reckoning up the sum he would be likely to make that day at Nottingham Fair by the sale of his pots and pans.

"Two dozen jugs should fetch four English crowns," he murmured, "and the red-clay jars are worth—"

"Now, how much are they worth?" said a voice in a laughing tone.

Peter looked up quickly. Six tall men in green were standing round him, blocking his path. All of them carried great bows, and the man who had spoken repeated his question again as Peter looked at him, and as he spoke his eyes lit up with laughter.

"How much are they worth, Master Potter?" he said. "I wonder" (with a chuckle) "if my master will know?"

Peter looked the six greencoats up and down with some interest.

"Is your master Robin Hood?" he questioned.

"He is," replied the smiling man, Will Scarlet, "and now he is waiting, as ever, at Robin Hood's Inn, for a visitor. Come along with us, master, and ye shall soon see him, I promise ye."

Peter stood on one foot, slowly rubbing his leg up and down with the other.

"I would like to," he considered in a doubtful tone, "but—" he looked at his wagon-load of pots rather ruefully, "I've these to sell in Nottingham town today, master. I fear I cannot stop."

"Well, then, I fear we must make ye," said Will Scarlet, still smiling, whilst his companions looked at the potter in some surprise. It was not often that chance passers-by, taken on the high road, showed a wish to be carried to Robin Hood's Inn. But, at a signal from Will Scarlet, they closed round the sturdy fellow and his wagon.

"Six against one," laughed Will. "Come, master, ye are no craven, I see, and I like ye for it, but ye are outnumbered this time, and my master is waiting."

"Oh, well,"—the potter gave up his wagon with a sigh—"since it must be so. But ye have made me miss the fair," he said.

All seven plunged into thc woods, and as they went, the potter, striding beside Will, chattered brightly of many things. He looked about him eagerly at the mighty trees, green and grand in all their summer splendour, at the long, majestic aisles of the forest, splashed with yellow sunlight, at the fresh grass carpeted with wild flowers.

"Master," he said at last, "I do not wonder now that your Robin Hood has chosen the greenwood for his home—'tis a sweeter place than the pleasantest castle that ever was built."

Presently, after half an hour's walk, they came to a clearing in the woods, where stood the outlaws' lodge. Peter, watching eagerly, saw a man coming out of the door to meet them, a brown-headed man in green, with a sword, and a shining horn at his belt.

"Here, master!" cried Will Scarlet, as soon as he caught sight of him.

"Is this the guest ye have brought me?" said Robin Hood. He came forward smiling. "Welcome, Master Potter!" he said. "Ye have many pots, I see, in your wagon. Have ye also money in your pocket?"

The potter had been staring earnestly at his new host ever since he appeared. But at the outlaw's words he stared the more, and then broke into a laugh.

"Money? Not I!" he said.

"What! Ye have none?"

"Not one groat. Why, master, was that what your fellows brought me here for? Ye thought I had money? Oh!" He shook with laughter, holding his sides. Then, making a sudden dive, he turned out all his pockets. "See!" he cried. "All empty! I've naught with me but the pots I was taking to sell at Nottingham Fair when your men met me. If they had taken me upon my homeward way, now, there might have been a different tale."

"Aye, there might," said Robin, laughing too. "Well, then, master, since ye have no money, I must demand your wares." He pointed to the loaded wagon. "Leave us these, for the use of my merry men and me—we are short of pots and pans—and I will let you freely out of the forest safe and sound."

Peter considered, scratching his head thoughtfully. It was an awkward business, certainly. He had started out that morning with his pots, meaning to make a good sum out of their sale before he returned from Nottingham Fair. Then the men in green had found him, and here he was before their master, and though the pots were to be taken from him, he was told that he might go free—on to the fair, or back to his home, as it pleased him. But he had no wish to go home penniless as he set out, and where was the use of going to the fair if he had nothing to sell? Peter wrinkled his forehead in perplexity, looking about him.

The outlaws were all around him, strong men and tall, watching him in some amusement and not a little wonder. Then he turned to their leader, standing with his hands on his sides, watching him too, his brown eyes twinkling. Somehow, after all, he liked the look of this Robin Hood, of whom so many tales were told. And Robin, looking him up and down, thought the same of the potter.

At last a light seemed to break in upon Peter. He lifted his head and spoke.

"I have heard many tales of you, Master Robin," he said, "and in all these tales it has been clear that you are a just and a true man. I have heard that you take from the rich and haughty man. That is right. I have heard also that you give to the poor man, and see that the poor man has his due. That is right again. Now, master, I am a poor man, with not many things in this world that I may call my own. I have no money in my pockets, but I meant to make a goodly sum out of my pots today. Now I am here, and they are here, and you say, since I have no money, you must take my pots from me. Will you listen to a plan I have? I am ready to fight, man to man, with one of your followers here." He looked round at the greencoats. "Choose which of them you will, I care not. I will meet him. If I beat him, you must let me and my pots and pans take our way in safety to Nottingham town. But if he beats me, master, then, all my wares are yours and his. Is it a bargain, say?"

"A bargain, and a fair one!" Robin's hand fell upon the other's shoulder heartily, and a cry of "Bravo, potter!" broke from his men. They crowded round Peter, patting him on the back, all talking at once.

"'Tis a fair plan," cried one.

"Aye, and a bold one, say I," added another.

"He's a sturdy fellow, master, this potter!" laughed a third.

"Stand round!" Robin ordered his men, and the outlaws closed together in a great green ring, Robin and Peter in their centre. A splendid set of men they were, the potter thought as he looked at them—broad-chested, strong, and muscular. Then he braced himself sturdily. He was ready to meet any one of them, aye, and to give a good account of himself too.

Robin's eye ran swiftly over the circle with a look of some pride. They were a company that any man might have been proud to own. Then his smile broke out as his glance rested upon a great black-haired man who stood directly opposite to him, between Midge the miller's son and the yellow-haired Allan-a-Dale.

Their leader lifted his finger.

"Little John, come forth!" he said, and John stepped into the ring.

"Here's your fellow, Master Potter," went on Robin. "Will he suit ye, think ye?"

Peter looked his big foe over coolly.

"Excellently," he answered, and turned to fling off his old brown coat and toss it aside, along with his battered hat. Little John threw off his own coat, and then stood for a moment looking down at the sturdy fellow from his own great height.

"Come on!" Peter cried impatiently. "What are ye waiting for?" Then, as the other put himself into position, he doubled his strong brown fists and made a rush at his foe. Robin Hood stepped back with shining eyes, and the circle of greencoats widened to watch the combat.

Little John was several inches taller than the potter, but the potter was broad and strong and quite fearless. Also, he knew how to fight. In vain, for some time, John tried to catch him off his guard, to drive a blow home. Peter defended himself well; nor was it all defence either, for already a stream of blood was pouring down John's cheek from a wound he had received.

Up and down they stamped and circled on the soft grass, with the ring of outlaws, silent and eager, looking on. But it was John's plan to tire out his foe, and at last he was beginning to succeed. Peter had received several hard buffets, and now was breathing fast, though he still struck out gallantly. At length he made a mighty lunge at the other, a lunge that was his last effort, for John met it with one doubled fist, and then, with the other, struck home, giving the potter so heavy a blow over his right ear that he was put entirely off his balance, and, stumbling backwards, fell headlong upon the grass. In an instant he was up again, panting out, "Come on!" whilst his foe stared in surprise, and the outlaws cried out in admiration. But Peter, undaunted as he was, was half-stunned and bleeding heavily from the recent blow; and a second buffet, dealt more gently this time from Little John, sent him again to the earth.

Robin stepped quickly into the ring again, and helped the fallen man on to his feet.

"Well done, potter!" he cried, whilst the outlaws called "Bravo!" again, and Little John came close.

"Ye are a gallant soul," he said. "I am sorry ye did not win. Will ye shake hands?"

"Aye, with all my heart!" Peter cried, and mopped his wounded head with one hand as he held out the other to the victor. Then he turned, picked up his coat, and got into it stiffly. "Ye fought finely," he added. "Well sirs, I'll leave ye my pots and pans and I'll be going." He staggered and swayed a little as he spoke, but immediately Robin's arm was about him, and the outlaw was leading him to a bank of moss under a tree near by.

"Sit you there," he said kindly. "We will talk of your pots and pans and of your going, in an hour or so. Here, Midge, fetch a bowl of water, and, the rest of ye, bring food and wine."

Peter leaned against the tree gratefully. "I thank ye, master," he said rather faintly. "My—my head's a-spinning like a top."

John took the bowl of water from Midge's hands, and, kneeling on the grass, began to bathe the potter's bruised head and face; whilst Allan-a-Dale spread a cloth beneath the tree, and set forth meat, bread, and wine.

They sat down to the plentiful meal, and Peter, revived by the good food and drink, was presently able to sit up and to talk.

After they had ended, Robin drew the potter into the lodge, and ten minutes later stepped out of it again—alone this time—but now he was wearing the potter's rusty suit of brown and the potter's old hat.

"What, master!" Will Scarlet as he saw him.

"Pray you, stand aside!" Robin waved them all away airily. "I am well-nigh dead for a frolic, and I am going to sell pots at Nottingham Fair."

"Ye are mad!" said J ohn. "Why, have ye thought of the danger? If ye were caught—Robin Hood of Sherwood!"

"Pooh!" His master moved to the potter's wagon and took up the shafts lightly. "I know well what I am doing, which I think is more than the good folk of Nottingham town will know, I promise ye. Oh, I shall make a rare salesman." He laughed, then jerked his head in the direction of the lodge.

"He'll be asleep by this, I'll warrant," he said, "he's well-nigh spent. Ye buffeted him harder than he'll admit, John. 'Tis a brave fellow, and we owe him something for treating him so. Well, fare ye well, lads. I'll be back at sundown, if I can keep out of Master Sheriff's way."

He nodded and waved his hand to the outlaws, and so, pushing the wagon before him, vanished down the nearest glade.

It was still two hours before noon when Robin arrived at the town, and the fair was in full swing. The market-place was filled with animals and people—horses, cows, pigs, goats, farmers, countrymen and countrywomen, knights, townsfolk, one or two friars in cowls and sandals, and here and there a finely dressed lady on horseback with her squire. Booths and stalls were set up all round the square; in one corner a quack-doctor bawled out the virtues of his pills at the top of his voice; in another a juggler and tumbler in pink spangled hose performed on his brightly-coloured carpet, the centre of an open-mouthed crowd. The air was full of sounds—clamour and laughter, cries of sellers and buyers, the grunting of pigs, the lowing of cattle.

Robin trundled his wagon boldly into the midst of the crowd—a tattered, jolly, dirty-faced fellow—jostling, pushing, laughing with the rest of them. At last he found an empty space in the centre of the square, with a gingerbread-booth on the one hand and the quack-doctor's stand upon the other, and here the outlaw halted and turned his wagon round.

Quickly he set out his pots and jugs and ranged them in rows; then, perching himself upon the wagon, his long legs dangling, he began to cry his wares.

"Pots to sell! Pots to sell! Pans and jugs, jars and bowls! Who'll buy? Who'll buy?"

His great voice rang out lustily, fresh and cheerful, above the clamour of the crowd, and at once many of the passers-by turned and stopped and then came near.

"Jugs, have ye?" cried a red-faced countryman, "the goodwife is needing some. Let me have a couple, master."

"Six groats a-piece," Robin cried. "Rare jugs they are and finely made. Do ye want a porridge-pot, mother?" He looked at a red-cloaked old dame who stood by. "Mine make the best porridge in all Nottinghamshire. A silver piece each, I pray ye."

"They're dear!" grumbled the dame, fumbling with her wallet. "Now, if that clumsy Moll had not broken my old one yesternoon—well-a-day!—'twas my grandmother's!"

"Saints! Then 'twas out of fashion," laughed Robin, "and I do not wonder that that Moll of yours broke it, mother. Take her this, instead, and tell her to have a care of it and I will come some day to taste her porridge out of it." The old dame put a coin in his hand, chuckling, then carried off her purchase as Robin lifted his voice again to cry: "Pots to sell! Who'll buy? Who'll buy?"

A crowd soon gathered round him, and presently he was driving a thriving trade. Folk loitered and listened to this busy pot-seller with his deep, jolly laugh and merry tongue, who praised his wares and jested with his customers and seemed to charm the money out of their very pockets. It was hard to keep from buying from so cheery a salesman, certainly, and Robin saw with delight that his stock was growing quickly less. Many passers-by looked hard at him, his laugh was so ready, his voice so loud, but no one seemed to know him.

By-and-by there was a stir in the crowd, and the folk parted to right and left as a brown horse came slowly through the market-place, bearing a short, fat, richly-dressed man on his back.

"The Sheriff! The Sheriff!" whispered the people, and the men doffed their hats. But the pot-seller took no heed. He was seated cross-legged on his wagon, and as the brown horse came by:

"Pots to sell!" he cried. "Pots to sell, Master Sheriff!"

and looked up into the rider's face with a pair of bright eyes that shone beneath his wide old hat.

The Sheriff drew rein, looking down. "Who are you, fellow?" he cried, but Robin only laughed and answered:

"Pots to sell, Sir Sheriff! Will ye not take something home for your lady? Here is one, now." He held up a quaintly-formed jug with a handle shaped like a bow. "See this!" he cried, "'twill set ye in mind of Robin Hood, the good bowman of Sherwood!"

The Sheriff took the jug in his own hands.

"What do you know of Robin Hood, potter?" he asked, frowning.

"What do I know?" roared the outlaw. "Why, that once he stole my pots from me, but I outwitted him for all that, for I carried them off again before his very eyes."

The Sheriff burst out a-laughing.

"Ye did?" he cried.

"Aye, that did I!" Robin replied, and joined in the laughter.

"Ye are a clever fellow," the Sheriff answered, "and I will keep the jug. Here!" And he tossed the pot-seller a gold piece and rode on.

The crowd closed again round Robin, more curious still. Many asked him questions concerning his adventure with the outlaw of Sherwood, to which Robin gave laughing answers; and the buying and selling went on swifter than before.

All through the day Robin remained at the fair, and by late afternoon, when the throng had grown less, his stock of pots had entirely disappeared, and the wallet at his waist was heavy and full. Mightily pleased with the result of his frolic, he made the weighty bag secure, jumped off his perch, and, shouting a cheery farewell to those who still lingered about him, seized his empty wagon and trundled it out of the town, whistling as he went.

He was still whistling when he came at sunset once more to his beloved Sherwood, and passed into the clearing before his woodland lodge. The low sun struck the trees into a glory of rosy hues and lit up the figures of his men and of the potter, who sat grouped on the greensward in the cool evening air.

Little John spied the wanderer first. "Back again, master!" he cried gleefully, and inwardly breathed a sigh of relief. He had been fidgety ever since Robin had left them. His master was such a freakish fellow, for ever running his head into danger, with a seeming indifference that sometime scared even Little John himself.

"Back again!" Robin echoed his words, smiling at Peter as he did so.

"Said I not that I would be back at sundown?" he cried. "And said I not that I would make a rare salesman for thy pots, good Peter? Oh, gather round, gather round, all of ye, for I have to tell ye of rare sport; of how the good folk of Nottingham clustered round me like bees round a honey-flower; and how I sold a jug to Master Sheriff (how ye stare, John!—aye, to Master Sheriff) for a gold piece; and how, in short, I made a pocketful o' money, enough to put any man in good humour for a month."

He flung himself on the grass, and Peter and the

outlaws gathered close to listen. So he told his tale, with much interruption from one and another, and many bursts of delighted laughter in between.

But when he had ended, he leaned over and put into Peter's hand the leather wallet with its heavy burden of coins.

"That's yours," he smiled. "Nay, Master Peter, no thanks. I said we owed ye something. Take it; I sold the pots in your place, man, and the sport I got out o' the business is payment enough for me. Here, John, take him to the edge of the forest, and see him safely on his way. And go ye with them, Midge, and wheel his wagon for him. Farewell, good Peter, and remember"—he leaned closer, his merry brown face alight with laughter—"remember, whene'er ye think of Robin Hood, that ye are not the only potter who has sold pots at Nottingham Fair."

11

The Black Monks

Alan-a-Dale and his wife were seated one day in the sunshine outside the hut that the outlaws had made for them. Robin had been back in the greenwood for a month now, after his stay in the fishing village, and life in the forest went on in the old merry way.

"I feel so lazy this morning," yawned Alan-a-Dale to Ellen. "Sing to me, Ellen, and lull my mind to sleep."

Ellen laughed.

"If I sang to you it would never send you to sleep! It would be more likely to drive you away!"

They became silent again, and would not have noticed Friar Tuck walking by their dwelling if he had not greeted them in his cheery, musical voice.

"Good morning!" he called. "I am off for a walk."

He would have strolled on, but Alan-a-Dale called to him.

"Wait for us, good friar," he shouted rising from the grass. "We will come with you."

The three walked on through the forest. They had not gone far along a leaf-strewn lane when they heard a peculiar sound.

"Quick—into these bushes!" gasped Friar Tuck.

The three dropped behind a bush. All was quiet again. Friar Tuck raised his head above the bush, and looked about him. Not far away he could see two black horses tethered to a beech tree.

"Strange!" he whispered, as he told Alan-a-Dale of his discovery. "Where are the owners of the horses?"

"That's something I'm going to find out!" remarked Alan-a-Dale.

"I beg your pardon!" said the friar. "You mean we!"

"All right," said Alan, with a smile. "Let us walk quietly over to the horses and see what we can find out."

They were joined by Ellen. As they neared the tethered animals, they heard soft chanting not very far away.

It was Friar Tuck who saw the figures first. He caught hold of Alan-a-Dale's arm and halted him.

"Look!" he whispered. "Look through the trees!"

Alan and Ellen looked. Standing in a circle of birch trees were three men in monk's habits. Two of them were black monks, the third was a mendicant friar. His gown was so dirty that Friar Tuck had difficulty in recognising the brown colour that showed him to be a friar like himself. Suddenly the three figures dropped down on their knees. The weird chanting that Friar Tuck and his friends had heard before broke the silence again.

"This is interesting," said Alan-a-Dale, softly. "Let's creep closer and listen to their chants."

The three crept silently nearer and hid themselves behind an oak tree. They could hear the words that the monks were chanting now.

"Money, money! Send us, oh, send us some money to serve our needs!"

They sang in a low, mournful tone. The watching outlaws could clearly see the faces of the two black monks, and their expressions were sad indeed. The mendicant friar, whose back was turned to the onlookers, sang with the most unhappy voice of all. Indeed, he was having great difficulty in keeping in tune with his fellows. Altogether it was a depressing gathering.

When the dismal chant for money was over, the mendicant friar stood up and addressed the two black monks.

"My brothers," said the friar sadly, his head shaking slowly from side to side, "we have no money. We have prayed earnestly for money to be sent us. Now our prayer is over." He hung his head in silence for a moment, then went on, with deep gloom in his low voice, "Let us search our pockets again and see what Heaven has sent us in answer to our prayers."

He looked first at one of the monks, who stood up and thrust his hands deep into the pockets of his gown.

"Alas, friar, I still have nothing!" he said.

The friar looked towards the second monk. He, too, rose and felt in his pockets. They were as empty as before.

Friar Tuck whispered to Alan-a-Dale and Ellen that the two black monks would be expected to give money to the mendicant friar if they had any on their persons. That was the custom, for mendicant friars were permitted to beg money from other people.

"It looks to me," Friar Tuck told the others in whispers, "as if the mendicant friar asked the two monks for money, and that they have been praying for some."

One of the black monks spoke again.

"As we told you before, friar, we were robbed this morning before you met us."

"It is true, friar," said the other. "We were caught by Robin Hood's men and robbed of all our money."

"Ah, but, brothers," broke in the friar, "though you were robbed this morning, you have since prayed for money. I feel sure that your prayers have been answered."

The two black monks looked sadly at each other. They began to wonder whether the mendicant friar was a little out of his mind.

"Perhaps," went on the friar, "it would prove more fruitful if we searched each other's pockets instead of our own!"

Again the two black monks looked at each other. What a pity they had bumped into the idiotic friar that morning, they thought. Nevertheless, they obliged by first searching the friar's pockets. They soon found that he was without a penny.

"Now allow me, good monk," said the friar, as he reached out his hands towards the first monk.

Suddenly silver coins began to rain from the monk's clothing, just as if he were made of coins. Coins fairly covered the ground at his feet. The friar then searched the second monk. The same thing happened. Coins began to pour down on to the grass about his feet. Each of the monks had been wearing a belt inside his cloak, and attached to the belt were a dozen bags full of money. The friar stepped back.

"Our prayers have been answered!" he exclaimed. "We did not ask in vain. And, since we promised one another that we would share what Heaven should send, here is a handful of coins for each of you."

The two monks gaped stupidly at the wealth lying on the ground. It was all money they had saved from collections in the Abbey, and they were taking it to a safe hiding-place. But there was little that they could say to the friar, for, having once told him that they had no money on their persons, they would be proved cheats if they tried to claim the money now.

"Take your steeds," said the friar. "Go your way in the knowledge that you have done a great deed of kindness on this memorable day."

They two monks shuffled away to the spot where their horses were tethered.

"Oh, and by the way," called the friar after them, "next time you meet a poor man, be sure to show him as much honest charity."

The monks made no reply. They mounted their horses, and made off into the forest.

The mendicant friar stood looking after them for a few moments, then he burst out laughing. As the mounted figures vanished into the greenwood, he took off his cowl and then stepped out of his long monkish habit. Underneath he was wearing Lincoln green!

The three watchers recognised him at once. He was Robin Hood!

Suddenly Robin turned in their direction.

"Lady Ellen! Friar Tuck! Alan-a-Dale!" he cried, still laughing. "Whatever are you doing behind that tree?"

The three looked guilty. Robin Hood walked over to them.

"I saw you come," he laughed. "Did you enjoy the fun? Come and help me to pick up all this wealth."

The three ran to help their leader pick up the coins

that the black monks had left behind.

"There must be well nigh four hundred pounds here," said Friar Tuck.

Well pleased with the morning's fun, Robin Hood and his friends strode, happily back to their camp, the richer by four hundred pounds.

12

The Two Strong Wills

Robin was walking along the Nottingham road one day when he saw two men coming towards him.

"Good afternoon!" said Robin to the men.

"I have no use for fellows who bow and scrape to me," said one of the men to Robin.

Robin was angered by the fellow's tone.

"Civility costs nothing," said he.

The man looked at Robin, as if to inquire what sort of man he was that should dare to answer him back.

"Any more insolence from you," said the man, "and I shall knock your head off!"

"You are welcome to try," said Robin.

He was not afraid of these two men. Many times had he had encounters with such ruffians, but he had always been able to give a good account of himself.

"Take care!" said the other man. "We are messengers from the Bishop of Hereford. We are on our way to Nottingham to deliver a message to the Sheriff. We do not intend to be hindered by such as you.

"But you are hindered, you see," replied Robin, with a smile.

The two men laughed. Just then Little John came up and asked Robin if he was having trouble. Robin told him that the two men were to spend the night with them, and Little John wasted no time in tackling one of the men. Robin went for the other. With their superior strength and training, the outlaws were soon escorting the two men back to camp.

An idea was building up in Robin's mind. Before they had reached the camp, he made plans for a new adventure.

The men were given food and then made to lie down with the rest of Robin's men, and so spend the night with them.

Early next morning, Robin called Will Scarlet and Will Gamwell.

"How would you like to carry out a dangerous piece of work for me?" asked Robin.

The two Wills were keen at once.

"What do you want us to do, Robin?" asked Will Gamwell.

"I have read the letter that those two messengers were taking to the Sheriff of Nottingham. In it the Bishop of Hereford is asking for a loan of two hundred pounds. He says that it is urgent and very important. Do you think that you two could impersonate the two messengers and go to the Sheriff with this letter? It would be such fun to disappoint the Bishop, and at the same time to score one against the Sheriff of Nottingham."

The eyes of the two Wills glistened.

They changed clothes with the two messengers, and, with the letter, set out for the Sheriff's castle. They arrived at Nottingham in the early afternoon and went straight to the Sheriff. He read the letter in silence.

"Two hundred pounds is a lot of money," he said. "If I scraped together all the money I have with me I doubt whether it would total that amount."

"Then we had better take as much money as you can gather," said Will Scarlet quickly. "The Bishop will be very angry with us if we go back to him with nothing."

The Sheriff at length agreed to gather as much money as he could, and collected altogether a hundred and fifty pounds. He gave this money to the two men.

"Be very careful," he told them. "There are men in Sherwood Forest who would not hesitate to rob you of all your money if they caught you. They are led by Robin Hood, the outlaw."

"We have heard of him," said Will Gamwell. "We have no fear of being caught and robbed."

They thanked the Sheriff, and walked out of his room. On reaching the gate, they came face to face with the Bishop of Hereford! The Bishop had come to the Sheriff personally because he was so much in need of the money that, after his messengers had set out, he thought a personal visit would make more certain of the required loan.

The two Wills did not wait. They took to their heels and ran out of the gate. But they had not gone far before the Sheriff learned from the Bishop's own lips that the two men were impostors. At once, the Sheriff, with his men, set out to catch the two fugitives.

"We shall never be able to get back to the forest," said Will Scarlet.

"Let us try to reach Sir Richard of Lea's castle," panted Will Gamwell.

The two men ran in the direction of Sir Richard's stronghold, and came at last to the gate. Sir Richard welcomed them, as men of Robin Hood's band. He had not forgotten the kindness shown him when he fell on hard times.

Not far behind the two runaways was the Sheriff. He called his men to the castle. There he decided to attack the main gate. He took his men some distance away to consider the best way of launching the assault.

Sir Richard guessed what his enemy intended to do. So he immediately ordered that the wooden planks of the drawbridge should be loosened so that they were just resting on their cross supports. The drawbridge was to be left down.

All this was quickly and efficiently done.

A few minutes later, a great force of the Sheriff's men charged towards the drawbridge. The Sheriff and the Bishop were in the lead. The Bishop had come racing up when he first saw the chase, and he had now joined in the fray.

They saw that the drawbridge had been left down, and thought that someone had blundered, for it was natural that it should be pulled up at the first sign of attack.

The Sheriff and the Bishop raced across the bridge, followed closely by the first of the force. From inside the castle Sir Richard's men began to raise the drawbridge. As the great structure rose upwards, the loosened boards began to slip. Very soon, as the angle of the bridge became steeper, the boards, with nothing to hold them, began to slide right off the bridge. With a great splash, they slid into the moat below. The mass of men on the bridge went down with them!

The Sheriff and the Bishop, who had reached the end of the drawbridge, were able to cling to the great iron gate and thus save themselves from falling into the water. They looked rather like monkeys hanging on to the gate!

Inside the castle Will Scarlet had made a great bucket of paste. Together he and Will Gamwell carried it to the room above the drawbridge and watched what was going on through the holes that were always bored in the floors of these chambers.

When they saw what had happened to the Sheriff and the Bishop, they poured the great bucket of sticky paste through the holes in the floor, right on to the heads of the two struggling men below.

The proud Bishop and the haughty Sheriff were smothered in the wet, sticky mass, which forced them to loosen their hold on the gate and slide down into the water.

Those inside the castle roared with laughter.

All thoughts of money were forgotten for the moment by the Sheriff and the Bishop. Their one concern was to reach dry land. They swam as strongly as they could for the far bank. Once upon dry land they ran as fast as they could towards the Sheriff's own castle. They had had enough for one day!

The two Wills dined with Sir Richard, and, after thanking him for his kindness in helping them to escape, they made their way back to Robin Hood and his Merrie Men.

13

The Rescuing of the Widow's Three Sons

"There are twelve months in all the year,
As I hear many say,
But the merriest month in all the year
Is the merry month of May.
With a link a-down, and a-day O
With a link a-down, and a-day.' "

Robin Hood was striding along upon the broad high road that led to Nottingham town, singing the words of his song in a clear, joyous voice.

The merry month of May had broken sweetly over fair England, and here was a glorious morning of sunshine and mild breezes after a long night of wind and rain. The sky was dappled with snow-white rolling clouds, with sheets of blue between, like azure lakes between snow-fields; the roadside grass, the trees, the hedges, were fresh and green as emerald. And sky and trees and hedges were mirrored, one and all, in the great pools left in the hollows by the road-side after the last night's rain.

Suddenly, from a broad meadow upon Robin's right hand, a lark sprang from its grassy nest and mounted high in the air, singing as it flew. The sweet, continuous song floated down to the man upon the road, and checked the tune upon his lips as he stood still to watch the bird until it vanished, a tiny speck, amidst the clouds.

"Ah!" he cried, "we know what it is, Master Skylark, do we not, to live a free and careless life in Merrie England all on a day in May? We know 'tis better to sing our matins under the wide heaven than to mumble them between four walls—eh, thou rogue? We know——"

The sound of sobbing near at hand brought him to earth again sharply, loud and piteous sobbing, with a note of distress in it that made Robin halt at once. He lowered his eyes and looked round. Ten yards away, upon a leaning milestone beside the roadway, a woman was sitting with bowed head, holding an apron to her eyes. She was grey-haired, and looked old, and she wore a neatly-patched cloak and a snowy cap, but the outlaw could make out nothing of her features, because her face was hidden in her apron.

He crossed the road quickly, however, and put a hand lightly upon one poor heaving shoulder.

"What is the matter, mother?" he said in a gentle tone.

The bowed figure sat up in a moment, and the dame, casting aside her apron, looked up at him, wet-eyed, in a startled fashion. Then next instant she had dropped her face into her apron again, and was sobbing harder than before.

Robin, somewhat taken aback by this fresh outburst, muttered: "Bless me!" in a puzzled tone, and watched her for a second, his lips drawn together in a faint whistle. Then he bent forward again.

"Why, mother, ye'll cry your heart out," he said with rough kindliness. "Come, come; there was never yet an evil under the sun that was mended by weeping. Tell me what ails ye, and doubtless I can help ye, if 'tis in my power."

Something in his coaxing tones seemed to soothe the woman, for presently the sobbing grew quieter, and she sat up, wiping her eyes upon her damp apron.

"So," said Robin, nodding, "that is better. Now tell me."

It was an odd thing about this Robin Hood that, finding any fellow-creature, man or woman, in trouble, he had only to say "Tell me", in those kindly tones of his, and soon the whole tale of grief or annoyance would be poured with a sort of relief into his patient ears. It was so now. At his "Tell me" the woman looked straight up at him, and then, with sobs still catching in her throat, she spoke.

"'Tis my three sons, sir—fine brave lads such as any mother would be proud to own—and all three of them—oh, all three of them!—are to be hanged this day in Nottingham town. Alas! Alas!"

Robin's brown eyes grew solemn.

"That is a bad business, mother," he said. "What have they done that they should meet their deaths so?"

But the woman could not answer him. She had burst out weeping afresh, and a storm of sobs was shaking her from head to foot. Nevertheless, Robin stood before her patiently until the flood of tears had passed again. Then he spoke once more.

"What have they done," he repeated, "these sons of thine? Have they set fire to parishes or villages? Have they slain any holy men? Have they robbed any women? Have they murdered any children?"

The woman looked up at him again. Then she answered solemnly:

"Sir, they have done none of these things."

"Saints! Then, what are they being hanged for?"

"For bearing their bows with Robin Hood the outlaw. For killing a few of His Majesty's deer in Sherwood Forest. For naught else. 'Tis the Sheriff's doing."

"Ah! That Sheriff!" Robin muttered, and ground his teeth.

The woman looked at him keenly, then next moment got to her feet, still staring hard.

"Why, sir, I surely know ye!" she burst out at last. "Tell me, are ye not Robin Hood himself?"

"I am he," answered the outlaw, and then looked at her closely in his turn.

"And I'll wager I've seen ye before, also," he cried. "Here, turn to the sun. Aye, I knew it!" He slapped one green-clothed knee. "Now, I mind the day when that same Sheriff's knaves were hard at my heels, and ye hid me in your house till nightfall, and so sheltered me, and fed me, and set me on my way again. Was it not so? Ah, dame, Robin of Sherwood hath a long memory for kindnesses done. Now tell me, at what hour are your three sons to die?"

"They're to be hanged at twelve," she answered dismally.

"So? Well, 'tis but nine o' th' clock yet. Take heart, mother. Much might happen within the next three hours. Farewell then, and remember, Robin Hood will never forget" He nodded several times, told her gently to go home, and then set off upon the road again.

Half a mile nearer the town he met an old man shuffling along by the hedge-side in the sunshine. The stranger wore a pilgrim's cloak, all travel-stained and patched, and a wide-brimmed palmer's hat. As he passed the outlaw he called "Good day, master!" in a high piping voice, and Robin stopped.

"Good day!" he said pleasantly. "What is the news of the town, good sir?"

The palmer ruffled his grey hair beneath his hat.

"Why, there's little new, master," he said slowly, "save that three men are to be hanged this day at noon for stealing. Had ye heard that?"

"Aye. They've made a stir, too" answered Robin, thinking of the weeping dame by the road-side.

"They have so," agreed the palmer, thinking of the Sheriff.

The outlaw looked his companion up and down, shrewdly.

"Will ye change garments with me, old man?" he cried, and seemed to grow suddenly excited. Then he made a dive in the wallet that hung at his waist, and brought forth a handful of silver pieces which he held out towards the other. "Here's ten shillings in good silver for ye, if ye will," he went on quickly. "Come, I think 'tis a fair bargain; what say ye?"

The old man looked hurt.

"Your clothes are good, master," he said in a gravely gentle tone, "and mine are old and shabby, though 'tis not my fault that they are so. Ye should not laugh an aged man to scorn—it is not right to make sport of me."

"Nay, I make no sport," cried Robin in surprise. "By

my faith, I am in earnest. See." He pulled a piece of gold from the bag at his side, and forced it into the palmer's hand. "Does not this prove it?" he said. And at sight of the gold the old man, after staring at him for an instant, agreed to his plan.

In five minutes the exchange was made, and Robin, shaking with laughter, was viewing his new suit in one of the wide mirror-like pools by the highway. An odd figure he cut in the palmer's shabby hose and worn shoes, in the cloak, patched in many places, that well-nigh covered him, and in the battered old hat.

"Saints! Here is a matter for fun!" he roared. "What a scarecrow am I turned into! 'Tis only the habit that makes a man what he is, surely. Well, Master Palmer, I thank ye heartily, and so—good day to ye!" He nodded over his shoulder, laughed, and plunged into a belt of wood upon the left of the road, striking out for Sherwood Forest.

The old man looked after him a moment, blinking, then he shuffled off upon his own way, in Robin's suit of Lincoln green, clasping his gold piece tight and muttering, as he went.

* * * *

It was ten minutes to noon, and in the market-place of the town a little crowd of people had gathered to see the hanging. Two high wooden poles, with a cross-beam and a dangling rope, stood in the middle of the market, and round this the folk had clustered curiously. Upon a wooden platform beside it stood the prisoners, three young men in green suits, their hands tied behind them, bareheaded, guarded by three of the Sheriff's yeomen. The Sheriff himself was there, fat and pompous as ever, astride his fine brown horse. But something had upset him, it was plain, for he mopped his hot brow continually, and sent half a dozen fellows scuttling out of the market-place upon swift messages, whilst he himself stood up in his stirrups, and ran his eye over the crowd eagerly. The folk, watching his anxiety, presently became excited too, and murmurs began to pass from one to another, so that soon the alarm became known. It was almost time for the hanging, and the hangman had not come.

Several minutes passed, whilst the people crowded together whispering, and the Sheriff watched them, a frown between his eyes. Soon the messengers returned, one by one, and, coming up to one brown horse, whispered, each one, something in the Sheriff's ear, who, as he heard it, frowned more than ever. Then, after a minute or so, he lifted his voice and spoke.

"Good people," he cried, "the fellow who was to have hanged these rogues, has not come, as ye see, nor is he to be found, though I have sent out searchers far and wide. One of you, therefore, come forth and perform his office. Let the man who chooses so to do, step forth, and he shall be rewarded."

The crowd rustled and murmured, muttering one to another in low tones, but no one stirred. The High Sheriff of Nottingham was by no means loved by the townsfolk; moreover, the widow's three sons, whom he now meant to hang, had been favourites of the people, and they were Robin Hood's men. Robin Hood was a rogue, to be sure, but a kind-hearted one, and most of the townsmen bore him no ill-will.

So now they stayed where they were, watching first the Sheriff and then his prisoners, and more than one man whispered to his neighbour that Jonas, the hangman, knew what he was about when he did not appear at the Lord Sheriff's bidding.

"He may seek for his hangman for me," muttered one fellow, "I'll have no hand in the business of hanging the sons of a poor widow."

"Nor I," answered his neighbour. "Ah! see, his lordship is growing angry."

And indeed the Sheriff's looks were getting blacker and blacker as he saw no one stepped forth to offer his services. His fat face grew purple with wrath.

"Oh, ye knaves!" he cried, and spluttered with temper. "Stand out, one of ye, I say—stand out! What! Will none of ye come forth?"

Still no one moved, and the Sheriff, watching them, burst forth again: "I will have the law upon ye all! I will send word to His Majesty! I will——" a sudden tweak at his cloak made him come to a full stop, and he looked down at once.

A man was standing at his horse's stirrup, an old man, grey-haired and bent, with a long grey beard. He wore an old patched cloak, patched hose covered his weakly-bending legs, his shoes were old and worn. He wore, also, an ancient wide-brimmed palmer's hat, and he carried a staff.

Now he looked up with blinking eyes into the Sheriff's angry face.

"Do you want a hangman, sir?" he lisped in a high, cracked tone.

"Yes—in haste," replied the Sheriff eagerly. The old man looked at him sideways with a silly smile, shuffling from one foot to the other.

"What'll ye give to a foolish old man who'll play the hangman for ye this day, then?" he questioned.

The Sheriff, gazing down at him, thought this old fellow was certainly half-witted—such a strange figure did he cut, and so oddly did he speak; but at all events he seemed willing to do what the Sheriff wished. That was enough. The people were watching the pair of them closely, and one or two began to smile. The Sheriff smiled also, in a satisfied way, and with the air of a very great man indeed, bent down from his saddle.

"I'll give you," he said, "two sets of clothes—new ones—for I think you stand in need of them, old man!—and thirteen pence besides. Will that satisfy you?"

The old man capered with delight, and so odd were his antics that the crowd rocked with laughter, whilst the Sheriff looked on in amazement.

"Thou art a nimble old fellow," he said in some surprise. "But come, to thy business now."

The other did not stir, however. Indeed; he seemed now to have forgotten the offer that the Sheriff had just made, for his eyes wandered round a little absently, and then all at once he laughed.

"Faith!" he chuckled; "I'm maybe not so poor as ye think, and, now I remember, I've ne'er played the hangman before in all my life. Nay, I'm not so poor, oh no! I have a bugle-horn, I——"

"Come, come," cried the Sheriff impatiently, "this

is foolishness, old man. I have no time for silly chatter. Get to your work."

"But my horn—my horn," persisted the old man. "Let me blow my horn. I will not play hangman for ye at all this day, unless ye let me blow my horn." He fumbled beneath his cloak and began to whimper, and the watching people whispered "He is crazy," but the Sheriff frowned.

"Have done with this fooling," he blustered. "Blow thy horn, madman, as hard as thou wilt, and then get to the hanging, and let us make an end of this business."

The old man stopped whimpering and began to prance again, whereat the crowd roared. Then he dived under his cloak, unfastened an old bag at his waist and brought forth a silver-mounted horn, tied with flowing green ribbons. The three prisoners on the platform craned their necks to see, and next moment looked at one another in open-mouthed surprise. They had seen that horn before.

But the old fellow heeded no one. He tip-toed up to the Sheriff, dancing, one brown finger upraised.

"Hark!" he quavered. "Hark to my beautiful horn!" then set it to his lips and blew.

"Come hither!" a long, loud summons sounding clear over hill and dale; *"Come hither!"* still longer and louder; and again, *"Come hither!"* until those in the crowd thrilled at the brazen notes. As they died away there was an instant's silence. Then "Look!" cried a lad's eager voice, and next moment the people were indeed looking with all their eyes, and my lord the Sheriff, gazing dumbly, felt a sudden chill of fear run

through him, for into the market-place, from every side, as if they had sprung from the very earth, flocked a flashing army of Robin Hood's merry men. Like leaves blown from the trees in autumn they swept and poured fast and thickly, surrounding the gaping crowd, the gallows, the platform, the Sheriff, the man with the horn.

The Sheriff himself lifted a trembling voice, which he tried in vain to make stern.

"Who are these?"

Then the palmer stood up straight, stepped forward, tossed his hat aside, and tore off grey hair and beard, showing to people and Sheriff the merry face and brown head of Robin Hood of Sherwood.

"They are my men," he said, and laughed a little, ever so softly. "And they have come to see justice done. Will that satisfy you?" He mimicked the Sheriff's pompous tones. Then he lifted his voice and spoke to the crowd.

"Begone!" he cried; "all of ye, upon the instant, as ye value your lives! Quick!" And the folk needed no second bidding, but one by one shuffled away.

Robin glanced round, and his eyes fell upon the three yeomen guarding the prisoners. "You also!" he called. "Hasten!" And the yeomen meekly followed the people.

At last Robin turned to the Sheriff, and looked him over coolly.

"I have the best mind in the world to hang you," he said.

In a moment the Sheriff was down from his saddle, and grovelling before the outlaw, cringing and mur-

muring. "Pardon, master!" he cried imploringly. "Ah! spare me, I pray you."

"Pooh! What a coward ye are!" said Robin. "Ye deserve a short shrift and a tight rope, let me tell ye." He looked down for a moment at the terrified creature; then bent, picked him up, dumped him into his saddle, and striking the horse with the flat of his hand sent it galloping out of the market.

"After thy knaves! "he roared; "and see that ye meddle no more with Robin Hood or any of his men!" Then he strode across to the prisoners, pulled out his knife, and cut the cords that bound them.

"Your mother has well-nigh wept her eyes out about this hanging," he said, laughing, "ye had best go home and comfort her."

And the widow's three sons obeyed him.

14

Little John's Adventure

"It is high time that Robin Hood was brought to justice!"

As the Sheriff of Nottingham looked out from a window towards Sherwood Forest, the thoughts that were so often in his mind came to the surface.

Not far away, in Sherwood Forest, Robin Hood was thinking of the Sheriff of Nottingham.

"It is high time the Sheriff was made uncomfortable!" he told himself.

He strolled around his camp; but he soon dismissed the Sheriff from his mind when the inviting smells of breakfast were wafted towards him on the breeze.

The two men were forever plotting against each other. The Sheriff was eager to bring the outlaw to the gallows; Robin Hood was constantly playing tricks on him, for the outlaw knew the hatred that the Sheriff had for him and his band.

When, therefore, Little John told Robin that he had thought of a new trick to play on the Sheriff, Robin was keen to hear about it.

"What is it all about?" he asked.

"It is my own scheme, master," replied Little John. "I would rather like to try it before I tell you about it."

Robin did not press his faithful servant. He knew

that Little John would tell him when necessary all about his plan. But he was surprised indeed when he awoke the following morning to be told that Little John was missing from the camp.

The giant had arisen early and made his way to the castle of Sir Richard of Lea.

"Good Sir Richard," said Little John when he was shown into the knight's room, "I have tired of life in the greenwood. I would like to join your service as one of your soldiers."

There was something in the way that Little John spoke that caused Sir Richard to doubt the genuineness of the outlaw's request. It was as if Little John had something up his sleeve. However, the good knight was pleased to have a man of such strength amongst his soldiers, and he allowed him to stay.

Little John became a popular man amongst the other guards at the castle. In less than a month he had become well known as the finest archer in Sir Richard's service.

It was not surprising, therefore, that when some sports were to be held in Nottingham Little John was the first to be chosen amongst Sir Richard's soldiers as a contestant.

"The man seems very eager to enter the shooting match," mused Sir Richard to himself. "I somehow feel that Little John has a secret reason for being in my service."

Dressed in scarlet livery, Sir Richard's archers, with Little John at their head, marched into Nottingham on the day of the sports, ready to try their skill in the shooting match. It would have horrified the people of the city if they had known that the giant who was soon outclassing everybody with marvellous feats with the bow and arrow was, in fact, one of Robin Hood's outlaws.

The Sheriff of Nottingham was amazed at Little John's skill, and he was excited when the time came for the presentation of prizes. There was no doubt about the winner.

"You have a fine aim," the Sheriff congratulated him, as he gave the prize to Little John. "I could do with you working in my service. How does that idea appeal to you?"

"I should like it very much, sire," said Little John, eagerly.

"What is your name?" asked the Sheriff.

"Er—Reynold Greenleaf," replied Little John. It was the only name that came to his mind.

Arrangements were made between Sir Richard and the Sheriff for the transfer of Little John's service from the knight to the Sheriff. Sir Richard was unwilling to allow his giant servant to serve under the Sheriff, but he caught the twinkle in Little John's eye, and guessed that this had been the outlaw's plan from the very beginning. It was all clear to him now, and he gave his permission for the transfer to take place.

"I will pay you double your present wage, Reynold Greenleaf," said the Sheriff. "You will be one of my archers—a high honour for any man. I will clothe you and find you lodgings and food."

So Little John entered the Sheriff's service, and, for a little while, all went well. But Little John was only awaiting an opportunity. He would strike at just the right moment.

He discovered that the Sheriff was a mean man to his servants. Few of them received their wages at the proper time. Their food was poor, and Little John remembered hungrily the great feasts he had enjoyed in Sherwood Forest. How he longed to rejoin Robin Hood and his Merrie Men!

"Reynold Greenleaf!" called the Sheriff one day. "I am going to a distant town with some of my men. You shall stay in charge of my castle until I return."

"Very good, sire," said Little John.

The steward, who had been left to feed the remaining guards, was a lazy man. He troubled little about the cooking, and he didn't offer Little John anything to eat at all.

On the day after the Sheriff had left, Little John entered the kitchen and saw the steward idly sleeping in a chair.

"I haven't had a bite to eat all day," said he. "Food I must have, Sir Steward, and I intend to have it now."

The steward awoke suddenly.

"Eh?" he asked, rubbing his eyes.

"I want some food!" growled Little John.

"Then get it," retorted the surly steward.

Little John made a grab at the steward, who fled towards the door. The outlaw sprang after him and knocked him down. The steward did not move after that. Little John helped himself to a fine meal.

"What's been going on here?"

The demand came from the doorway. Little John glanced slowly round. Leaning against the doorpost was the burly figure of the cook.

"I felt hungry," said Little John, in a matter-of-fact

tone. "The steward told me to get my own food. So I did."

"What is the steward doing on the floor?"

"Oh, he kept getting in my way," laughed Little John.

The cook took down a large staff from the wall and set about this new servant. He guessed what had happened. The greedy man had knocked out the steward and had stolen some food! Little John saw the cook grab the staff. He, too, found one, and they set about each other, giving blow for blow. After half an hour they both paused for rest.

"You're a strong fellow," said Little John, "and brave as well."

"You're not so helpless yourself!" returned the cook.

"If you can shoot as well, why not come with me and join Robin Hood and his Merrie Men?" suggested Little John.

"And who are you that you can make such an offer?" asked the cook curiously.

"Men call me Little John," was the reply.

He told the cook how he had become one of the Sheriff's archers. The cook laughed at the joke.

"I'll go with you," he decided. "The life would appeal to me. But we must go at once before the steward here wakes up."

"Yes," agreed Little John, "but we can't go empty-handed. The Sheriff owes me some wages."

"He owes me some, too," said the cook.

"Then let's pay ourselves, and charge the Sheriff interest," laughed the outlaw.

They strode to the Sheriff's private room and broke open desks and drawers. They gathered together a great bag of gold, and took all the Sheriff's silver dishes. These they crammed into two sacks.

"Robin Hood will have dinner in style today!" chuckled Little John, as the two made their way through the forest.

At length they came in sight of the outlaws' camp deep in the greenwood. The Merrie Men were seated round their camp fires.

"Why, look who's here!" gasped Robin, springing to his feet as his old friend returned.

The two men staggered towards Robin with their loaded sacks over their shoulders.

"Hello, master!" called Little John.

"What are you doing in the Sheriff's colours?" asked Robin.

"Oh, I'm one of the Sheriff's men. At least, I was until a short time ago."

Robin laughed heartily when he had heard the whole story.

"When the Sheriff returns he will be in a rage fit to shake the city of Nottingham!" laughed the outlaw leader. "Something tells me that we shall have a visit from him before long."

Robin was right!

15

Vengeance on Guy of Gisborne

"It's no good going to Gamwell Hall, Robin," said the old lady as she stopped working at her spinning wheel to face the outlaw.

"Why not?" asked Robin, stretching himself lazily in the woman's old fireside chair.

He had visited this aged friend while he was near Nottingham, and had told her of his intention of going to Gamwell Hall.

"Because it doesn't belong to Squire Gamwell any longer," was the old lady's reply.

"Indeed?" cried Robin. "But what of Maid Marian, and Will Gamwell? I promised Maid Marian that I would return, and return I shall!"

"Squire Gamwell is dead," said the old lady, quietly. "Sir Guy of Gisborne lives in the old Hall now."

Robin could hardly believe her. It was not the knowledge that the kindly old squire had died that disturbed him; it was the news that Sir Guy of Gisborne, a knight hated by Squire Gamwell, should be in residence.

"But surely Squire Gamwell would have left the Hall to his own son?" questioned the outlaw.

"Ah, he would have done if he could."

"What do you mean?"

"It was like this, Robin," the old woman continued,

"Sir Guy of Gisborne attacked Gamwell Hall in great force one day. There was a terrific battle, and it ended in the Squire being killed and the Hall taken by Sir Guy."

"What happened to Maid Marian?" was Robin's quick question.

"I don't know," replied the old woman. "Nobody knows."

"You mean to say she has vanished?" Robin was astounded.

"Some say she was away at the time of the attack. Some say Sir Guy of Gisborne held her prisoner and married her. Some say he killed her."

Robin stared blindly out through the window. Could it be true that Maid Marian—his Maid Marian—was dead? No! That could never be. He reeled out into the sunlight. Revenge against Sir Guy of Gisborne filled his mind.

When he returned to his greenwood camp, he called about him all his men.

"We are going to attack Gamwell Hall," he announced. "Sir Guy of Gisborne has captured the Hall and killed our friend, Squire Gamwell. What has become of Maid Marian and Will Gamwell nobody knows. We are going to find that out."

"What plans have you, master?" asked Little John.

"None, except that we attack tonight!"

It was dark that night. As Robin's men set out through the forest they talked excitedly amongst themselves about the daring attack they were about to make. Robin led them to the outskirts of the greenwood, across fields, and along darkened country lanes. At last the lights of Gamwell Hall could be seen in the distance.

"Quiet, men," ordered Robin. "Not a word until we have reached the Hall."

All speech ended. Only the soft tread of stealthy footsteps could be heard on the night air.

"Here's the moat," whispered the outlaw leader, as the party halted on the bank and looked carefully around them.

The cold dark water, rippling now and then as the breeze touched it, looked forbidding as some of the lights from the Hall sent shafts of yellow through it.

"Little John and Will Scarlet," breathed Robin, "I want you to swim the moat and then to creep up to the windows. Find out what is happening in the Hall and return to us. We shall cross the moat while you are gone and we'll meet you on the far side."

Little John and Will Scarlet slipped into the deep water and swam silently away from the party of men. They were not gone long. Robin's men had crossed the moat and were silently waiting on the other side of the water when the two men met them.

"Sir Guy is holding a feast," reported Little John. "They are making merry."

"That's lucky for us," said Friar Tuck. "It will be Robin Hood and his Merrie Men against Sir Guy and his Merrie Men."

"They will not be so merry when they have felt our steel," said Robin. "Now," he added softly, "advance through the fence."

Friar Tuck was the first to attempt to get through the fence. There was a hole in it, the hole that Little John and Will Scarlet had climbed through. But Friar Tuck was a man of very different proportions. His head and shoulders were through before he realised that his great girth would not allow the rest of him to follow. He was pulled back by those behind him The fence was torn down bit by bit until a hole large enough for the men to climb through in pairs was made.

"I'm going alone to the door of the Hall," said Robin, when all the men were standing in the grounds. "Keep silent and follow me in the shadows."

Robin went on ahead. He reached the door, and knocked.

"What do you want?" asked the doorkeeper, peering through the darkness at his visitor.

"Is Sir Guy at home?" asked Robin.

"He is."

"Then tell him that Robin Hood has come to see him."

Amazement showed on the doorkeeper's face as the light from inside the Hall fell on his rugged features. He took a step backwards. Was this really Robin Hood in person?

"I—I'll tell Sir Guy," he stammered. "Are you alone?"

"Do I look as if I have anyone with me?"

Again the doorkeeper peered into the night. He could see nobody.

"Wait!" he said.

He ran into the Hall and told Sir Guy of Gisborne.

"Robin Hood, eh?" laughed Sir Guy. "Tell him to come in."

"But he cannot be up to any good, sire."

"If Robin Hood wants to put his head in a noose, let him do so," shouted the knight.

"I fear he has some trick up his sleeve."

"Admit him, I say!" cried Sir Guy, smiting the table with his fist.

The doorkeeper said no more. He went back to the entrance and opened the door again. While he had been talking to Sir Guy, the rest of Robin's men had been slowly creeping towards the leader. Now they were all standing waiting at the door.

"You may enter," said the doorkeeper. "Sir Guy will see you in the Hall."

"Then out of our way," cried Robin, thrusting the man aside.

The Merrie Men followed Robin down the Hall to where Sir Guy was feasting at a trestle table with many knights. Around the walls were posted a number of Sir Guy's soldiers.

"Who gave leave for all those men to come in?" demanded Sir Guy. He had expected the outlaw to come alone down the Hall, and here he intended to insult him before taking him captive. But the sight of all Robin's archers made him rise up in terror.

"Villains!" he screamed. "Let not a single man remain!"

"Every man for himself!" shouted Robin, and dashed through the Hall towards the knight.

A terrific fight followed. Sir Guy's men were in the best position, for they had swords and battle-axes. These were more suitable for close-quarter fighting. But Robin and his men were strong, fresh and determined.

The two sides charged into each other furiously. Sir Guy's soldiers were brave and strong; they were used to fighting. But Robin's men were hardy, and they had sprung a great surprise by their sudden arrival. Robin's words of encouragement rang in their ears as they sprang forward to attack. Whenever one of Sir Guy's soldiers fell, his sword was snatched by one of Robin's men. The soldiers were no match for the determined men from Sherwood Forest, and soon they were falling back before the outlaws.

Suddenly Robin Hood cried a warning. An oil lamp he had seen swinging dangerously as a sword crashed into it suddenly fell to the floor. Another followed. Then another. The Hall was rapidly getting darker as lamp after lamp crashed to the floor.

Robin was still grappling with Sir Guy of Gisborne when the last of the lamps was hit and the Hall was plunged into darkness. In that moment Sir Guy acted with great cunning. In the confusion, he slipped free of Robin and made for the door of the Hall. In the darkness it was impossible to follow him. Neither side could tell who was who.

Suddenly fire flared up. One of the oil lamps had set light to part of the timbered wall of the Hall. The flames spread quickly. The whole building would be burning before long. Robin called his men together.

"Sir Guy has escaped," he shouted. "It's useless fighting on in this inferno. We must leave these rascals and return to the forest."

As the flames spread, Robin's men made their way out of the burning building and crossed the grounds to the moat. Some were being helped along by others. Two of the men had to be left behind. They had been killed by the soldiers.

"This is a sad sight," murmured Robin to Friar Tuck, as they stood for a moment on the other side of the moat, watching the flames leaping high into the air. "The gallant Gamwell Hall that I have loved for so many years will soon be no more."

But Robin's mind wandered from the Hall. He had set out to rescue the beautiful Maid Marian from Sir Guy of Gisborne; yet he had seen no sign of her.

"One thing is certain," he reflected. "Maid Marian was not at the Hall tonight. Even if she were in another part of the building she would have come to find out the cause of the uproar."

Then he thought that perhaps the story that Sir Guy had killed Maid Marian might be true, after all. What of Will Gamwell, too? These were disturbing questions.

As he wandered-deeper into the forest towards his encanlpment, he asked himself again and again, "Where is Maid Marian?"

The answer to that question came some days later.

16

Capture and Escape

Sir Guy of Gisborne returned on the following day to Gamwell Hall. As his horse drew near, the knight's face suddenly went white. There was no Hall. Only a smoking ruin stood before him, a ghastly reminder of the cost of his fight against Robin Hood.

"He's scored a great victory over me," fumed Sir Guy, seething with anger. "There's only one fitting revenge for this—the death of Robin Hood!"

He set off to visit the Sheriff of Nottingham. Together they should be able to work out a satisfactory plan. Sir Guy did not receive much encouragement at first from the Sheriff.

"I've been trying for so long to bring Robin Hood to the gallows," he said, "that I sometimes wonder whether the man is bewitched."

"He's no more bewitched than you or I," returned Sir Guy. "The secret is that he's got to be captured by cunning. He is too bold and clever to be taken by a straightforward attack."

"Then what do you suggest?" queried the Sheriff, keen to try anything that would bring his foe to the scaffold.

"I'm going to disguise myself as a traveller," said the knight. "I intend to set out alone into the forest, and by hook or by crook I shall find Robin Hood's camp. There I shall deal with the man in his own way," he said, determinedly.

"He has so many ways of his own," the Sheriff warned him.

"Do you not know that I am about the best swordsman in the country?" Sir Guy boasted.

"I have heard it said," admitted the Sheriff.

"That is how I shall fight Robin Hood—with my sword. But I shall bring him to you alive—at the sword's point! So you can have the gallows prepared for my return."

"How shall I know you have been successful?" asked the Sheriff.

Sir Guy thought for a moment.

"I will tell you," he said. "When I have captured Robin Hood I will blow a long note on a hunting horn."

The Sheriff did not share Sir Guy's confidence. Nevertheless he agreed to the plan and promised to listen for the sound of the horn.

The knight wasted no time. He arranged for the clothes of a traveller to be brought to him, and, slinging the hunting horn round his neck, set out alone into the forest.

Robin, in his greenwood camp, had asked Will Scarlet and Little John to go into Nottingham that same morning to buy some new green cloth.

"The fight of last night has torn many of our uniforms," he said. "These must be renewed at once. Most of them were worn out even before the fight."

Little John and Will Scarlet, disguised as poor travellers, parted a short distance before reaching Nottingham, so that no suspicion would be aroused. Will Scarlet bought a large quantity of the green cloth from a merchant in the city. He regretted his action almost at once, for he could sense that the man was suspicious of this poor traveller buying such a large amount of green material. Will Scarlet left the shop and hurried away.

As he looked back, he saw the merchant running across the road.

"The Sheriff will know all about me in a very short time," Will said to himself. "Now I come to think of it, I should have bought small quantities of the stuff at different shops so as not to arouse suspicion. However, it's too late to worry now."

The merchant did not stop running until he came to the Sheriff's office. He told his tale almost before he had recovered his breath.

The Sheriff ordered some of his men to chase the outlaw, passing on to them the merchant's description of the man.

That was the sight that met Little John's eyes as he entered the town. Having taken a different route, he was a long way behind Will Scarlet. But as he strolled along the city road, disguised as a traveller, he gasped as he saw his friend being chased by six of the Sheriff's men.

"Great heavens!" cried Little John. "He'll never outdistance those men if he holds on to all that cloth."

Though Will Scarlet's bundle of cloth was hindering him, he was making good progress. He was very fleet of foot, and now he was running for his life. The added weight began to tire him, and before long one of his pursuers began to gain on him. Suddenly Will stopped dead.

"Ah, my good comrade is caught!" murmured Little John, wondering how to act to aid Will Scarlet.

But Will was not at the end of his resources. He dropped his bundle, put an arrow to his bow, and, turning, shot the nearest of the runners through the heart. This was quickly followed by a second arrow. Another man dropped. Will picked up his bundle of cloth and ran on again. His pursuers stopped when the second man fell.

"Good shooting!" cried Little John, happily, quite forgetting himself in the excitement of watching his escaping friend.

It was Little John's bad luck that the Sheriff should be coming down the road at that moment. He heard the outlaw's cry.

"Good shooting, eh?" he echoed. He turned to the men who were with him. "Catch that man!" he yelled, pointing to Little John. "He's one of Robin Hood's men, too, I'll swear!"

Little John ran off. It was no use seeking to put up a fight in such a crowd. He ran swiftly, but the Sheriff's men closed in on him from all directions. At last he was tripped, and fell headlong to the ground. He put up a terrific struggle, but despite his great strength his captors were too many for him.

With his hands bound tightly behind him, Little John was led up a hill. The Sheriff came up to him.

"Good shooting!" he sneered. "I'll show you what's good for you." He turned to his men. "Hang this dog," he said. "Hang him now as a proof to the people that I mean business with Robin Hood's band."

Little John laughed in the Sheriff's face. He realised that his last moment had come. He determined to face death as he had faced life. He did not flinch as the rope was made ready to be placed around his neck.

In the distance a horn was heard. It gave one long clear note. The Sheriff knew what that meant. It signified that someone even more important to him than Little John had been captured. This was indeed a black day for the outlaws!

"This is indeed a great day," he said to his men. "You heard that horn? It was a signal arranged by Sir Guy of Gisborne and myself. It means that he has captured Robin Hood."

"Now, dog," sneered the Sheriff, turning to Little John, "you and your master will hang together."

John did not move. The news that Robin was captured came as a terrible blow to him. But he did not let the Sheriff see his feelings.

"Ha!" he laughed at the Sheriff. "You couldn't hang Robin Hood even if you had a thousand men with you."

Brave words, these, but Little John's stout heart was heavy.

Sir Guy came into view. He was dragging Robin Hood along with him. The ragged outlaw looked as if he had had enough. It was a sorry sight for Little John to watch, even in his last moments.

The two men advanced to where Little John stood with the Sheriff and two hangmen.

"Good work, Sir Guy!" cried the Sheriff.

Suddenly, Sir Guy of Gisborne threw off his cloak. The Sheriff stared, his eyes goggling. It was not Sir

Guy of Gisborne. It was Robin Hood himself! The man beside him was Will Scarlet.

There was no time for explanations to Little John. Robin cut through his bonds, and the three men fought their way through the crowd. The Sheriff and his men were too taken aback to act in time to prevent the escape of the three outlaws, who reached the safety of the forest in which they had their home.

They slowed down to a walk.

"But, master," cried Little John, breathlessly, "how did you manage to put over such a bold scheme? It was my blackest moment. I really thought it was the end of me—and of you."

Robin told him.

He had been walking along the Nottingham road, as he often did, when he came across an old traveller. In the conversation, the traveller was very inquisitive and asked him many questions.

"Does Robin Hood live in these parts?"

"I believe he lives in the forest near here," was Robin's reply.

"I seek him," said the stranger.

"So do many people," the outlaw answered.

"But I shall catch him. Do you see this sword? Do you see this shining mail under my clothing. I am no traveller. Sir Guy of Gisborne is as clever as the foe he hunts."

"Wonderful!" smiled Robin, with mock admiration in his voice. "But suppose you meet Robin Hood with all his Merrie Men?"

"Ah! I have thought of that. Do you see this horn? Some short blasts will warn the Sheriff of Nottingham that I need his help."

"And when you capture the outlaw—what then?"

"One long blast will tell the Sheriff to prepare the gallows."

"A clever scheme," said Robin. "But it's too bad of me, Sir Guy; I should have introduced myself to you before."

Sir Guy of Gisborne turned quickly. He realised that he had not been as clever as he thought.

"I am Robin Hood," laughed the outlaw.

Robin told Little John of the furious fight that followed, and of its end, when Robin had thrust his sword through the knight's heart, killing him.

Will Scarlet took up the tale.

"When I escaped from the Sheriff's men," he began, "I stopped some way along the road and turned to see if I was still being followed. It was then that I saw you, Little John, being prepared for the hanging. I ran quickly to tell Robin, and to my great relief I saw our leader standing over the dead body of Sir Guy. He quickly put on Sir Guy's clothes, and we came back, as you saw, to your rescue."

The three comrades walked on into the forest. Once again the Sheriff of Nottingham had been foiled.

17

A Greenwood Wedding

All this happened the day after the burning of Gamwell Hall. Robin was still worried about the fate of Maid Marian. He loved the girl dearly and had thought many times of asking her to marry him; but he knew that the life he was leading was no life for a young lady of gentle upbringing. He felt it would have been unfair to ask Maid Marian to share his forest adventures.

If Robin had only known Marian's true feelings he would have acted differently. She was in love with Robin, just as he was with her, and would have followed him to the ends of the earth if he had asked her. But she believed that he preferred to live a wild life with his men in the forest.

When Sir Guy of Gisborne attacked Gamwell Hall, Maid Marian and Will Gamwell, Robin's boyhood friend, had both been away visiting relatives. When they returned to find the Hall burned down and Squire Gamwell killed, they realised that now they were without a home at all. What could they do?

"I shall avenge my father's death," said Will, grimly.

"How can you?" asked Maid Marian, and there was little hope in her voice.

"I shall join Robin in the forest," he declared.

"Oh, Will, that is indeed the right thing to do," said

Marian eagerly. Her eyes brightened at the thought. She was silent for a moment. Then, at length, she looked up at her cousin: "Will!"

"Yes, Marian?"

"Take me with you into the forest."

"What?"

"I want to go with you. I want to—to join Robin Hood, too."

"But that is impossible. What could a girl do in the greenwood? It's a hard life, you know."

"It is no harder than living without a home."

Will did not reply. Maid Marian had lost her parents, her home. everything. Will knew that she loved Robin. Perhaps, after all, it would be the best thing of all—as long as Robin thought so, too.

"What will Robin say?" he asked the girl.

"We will surprise him," she replied, smiling.

They said no more. They packed their few belongings and entered the forest that afternoon. It was early evening when they came into Robin Hood's camp.

"We have visitors, master!" called Midge-the-Miller's son, as he saw the two figures approaching.

Robin came into the glade.

"Marian!"

The outlaw's face broke into a happy smile as he ran to meet the girl he had long wanted to see again. He was so eager to hear all that they had done since he last saw them that it was some time before Will and Marian could tell him of their decision to join the Merrie Men. Robin's face became serious when finally they were able to tell him their news; but he was only serious for a moment. His secret hope that Marian would one day join him was realised.

"Let me show you how we live," he invited them, proudly.

He took Maid Marian and Will round the camp, pointing out to them various members of the band, and showing them how the food was prepared, where they ate, and how the Merrie Men spent their time. Maid Marian and Will were fascinated.

Marian said that she, like Robin, could be happy in the forest. She soon settled down to life in the greenwood, and quickly endeared herself to the outlaw company. Robin Hood and she were specially happy together, and spent pleasant hours in close company in the forest.

What was more, the lost fortunes of Gamwell Hall had altered Robin's view towards marriage. Marian wanted Robin as a husband, and the two decided that they should marry and go on living in the forest together.

The wedding was fixed for an evening in spring. Robin and Marian stood under the fresh green leaves of a tall oak tree. Above them the green-leaved branches hung gracefully down, like the tracery roof of a cathedral. Birds sang in the boughs.

Friar Tuck stood in front of the couple, and around them the Merrie Men were grouped in silence. Marian had made a wedding dress for herself, and she looked beautiful as she stood quietly on the green and brown carpet of the forest by the side of her lover. Robin's men had smartened up their clothes of Lincoln green for this great occasion. Little John and Will Scarlet were in the forefront of the company.

When the marriage ceremony was over, the Merrie Men sang a hymn, their voices ringing bravely through the greenwood. Robin kissed his bride. Marian was now his wife. His greatest ambition had been achieved.

Twang!

An arrow whizzed through the air and embedded itself in the tree behind Robin and Marian. The peaceful scene was shattered. Who had shot the arrow?

"Whoever winged that arrow shall die!" cried Robin. Quickly he entrusted Marian to the safety of a group of his men. "Guard her with your lives!" he commanded.

He ran through the greenwood. Some distance away, he saw a strong band of the Sheriff's men. They had crept up silently, guided by the outlaws' voices raised in song. Robin could see them easily now through the trees. Their bright-coloured coats made a sharp contrast against the forest shades.

It was a desperate situation for Robin Hood and his followers.

Only twelve of his men were armed. They could not easily be seen amongst the trees because of their suits of Lincoln green, but that was the only advantage they had now that the Sheriff's men had sprung a surprise.

Robin decided at once on a bold plan. The Sheriff, unwisely, had arranged his men in one long line. This Robin noticed, and he was going to try to turn it to advantage.

"I want the twelve archers to line up, not too close to one another," he said. "Three unarmed men will stand behind each archer."

The men took up their positions quickly and silently.

"The archers shall shoot steadily. Each arrow must find a mark. As soon as any archer is tired his place shall at once be taken by one of the waiting men."

The men understood the plan, and, at his order, let their arrows fly. Thus Robin kept up a continuous barrage of arrows, and the Sheriff, not being able to see the men clearly, thought a huge force of Robin's men was hidden there.

All the outlaws were trained marksmen, and not an arrow was wasted. The Sheriff watched his soldiers falling one by one. There was nothing for it but to retreat. When an arrow pierced his hat he waited no longer. He turned his horse round and galloped away. This was a signal to his men, who stopped shooting and fled.

"Shall we follow them, master?" cried Little John.

"No!" replied Robin, with a smile. "Have you forgotten, Little John, that this is my wedding day?"

18

The Coming of Richard the King

Nottingham town was holding high festival, for the gallant Richard, the Lion-heart of England, had come to pay a visit there. and, with a few lords and chosen gentlemen of his household, was staying at the castle.

For word of Robin Hood's doings, and of how he ruled it in Sherwood Forest, had spread even to London town, and the tales of the outlaws' wild and merry adventures had tickled His Majesty's fancy greatly, so that he longed at last to see them, these children of the woods, in their forest home.

Therefore, he had come to Nottingham, but as yet he had seen nothing of Robin and his men. For the outlaws, unless they cared to seek for adventures which called them far away, were well enough content to keep within their own greenwood, and so great a love had Robin grown to have for his Sherwood that he rarely left it.

"We might as well have stayed at home," grumbled His Majesty one evening at supper, "for not so much as the tail of this rogue Robin's green coat do we see. The townsmen—good souls!—are beginning to weary me with their feasts and revels, and I long for something fresh. Why doth he not come to town?"

"The townsfolk would, perchance, not make themselves so civil to him as they are doing, to Your Majesty," laughed a black-eyed knight at the King's left hand. "I think, from what I have heard, that he is wise to stay away."

The King looked down the long table a little absently. "You are right, Sir Faulk," he said, "and, after all, who would exchange the greenwood for any town, if he were free to have his will? But—heigh-ho!—I would like, all the same, to meet with this Robin Hood?"

"Well, then, sire," answered Sir Faulk sagely, "since the fish will not come to the bait, the bait must go a-seeking for the fish."

"Hey?" cried Richard, and his eyes brightened.

"Listen to my plan, sire," the young knight replied, "and then, if ye like it. carry it through."

And, amidst the chuckles of the company, he began eagerly to unfold his new idea.

* * * *

Next morning broke, fresh and sunny, in the glades of Sherwood Forest, and Robin and his men, as was their way, were early astir.

About ten o'clock, Robin and some of his band had posted themselves in the shady woods that fringed the broad public highway which ran through the forest; for the coffers at the outlaw's woodland lodge were fast growing empty, and, as Robin observed significantly, 'twas high time some rich passenger filled them for him again.

For half an hour the men in green crouched low behind trees and bushes, their eyes upon the white roadway, their ears strained to catch every sou nd.

Presently, however, the distant clatter of hoofs upon the road, far off, made every man raise himself, and listen even more keenly than before. The woodlands seemed to rustle with excitement; the men in green felt for their bows.

"Rich folk!" whispered Robin to Allan-a-Dale who crouched beside him, "since they come upon horses. Now, maybe——"

Thirteen white horses trotted into view as he spoke, and upon the back of every horse sat a monk. At once Robin rose to his feet, swiftly and softly, giving a long clear whistle, and next moment the outlaws had flocked forth upon the highway, blocking the travellers' road.

The thirteen steeds came to a standstill, and Master Robin Hood looked their riders up and down. The foremost one, he decided at once, was some abbot, for his tall white horse had white-and-gold trappings, with fanciful bells upon the bridle, and the rider himself was clad in a rich robe of crimson silk, with a hood of the same shade. Beneath the cowl Robin caught sight of a pair of bright blue eyes, a smiling mouth, and a short yellow beard. The stranger looked at the outlaws in a curious fashion, and his followers did the same.

Robin Hood stepped forward, very straight and tall, and took the white horse sharply by the bridle.

"Hold, Abbot!" he cried, "and dismount—you and your men—for know that I am Robin Hood, and I have a mind to see the insides of your purses, aye, without delay."

"Master—" began the man in crimson silk, but Robin held up his hand.

"You had best make no trouble, Sir Priest," he said, "but hand over the money quietly—you will find it best. Bah! The presence of such as you sickens me! What business have you to ride abroad, all so rich and fine, upon the King's highway, with not one thought for poorer folk than you? Such nobles as you, with your pomp and finery, are a blot upon this good old England of ours. Come, your purse, sir!"

"Our master's tongue hath an edge upon it this morning," muttered Will Scarlet to John, but the other hushed him, watching the abbot.

The latter seemed neither alarmed nor offended at the outlaw's angry speech. Instead, he leaned from his saddle eagerly, looking down at the flushed and angry Robin Hood.

"I have no doubt that you speak truly, master," he said in a pleasant voice. "Many a time, indeed, have I found it irksome to be rich. But we are the King's own men—his messengers—and His Majesty waits, not so far away, to see the famous Robin Hood of Sherwood."

Robin's face changed on the instant. He let go the horse's bridle, stepped back, and bared his comely brown head to the sunshine.

"God save the King!" he cried in a loud voice, and immediately his followers took up the cry, "God save the King!"

"And all his well-wishers! "added Robin, smiling now. Then he looked round, half-fiercely. "May ill befall any that would deny his gracious sovereignty!" he cried.

The abbot gave a little laugh. "Then thou wishest thine own self ill," he said, "for dost thou not thyself deny him—deny his sovereign sway? Art thou not an outlaw, a rebel, a robber?"

"Now, by my head!" Robin cried, blazing up again. "Sir Priest, an' ye were not one of the King's own messengers I would tell ye that ye lied! For though I am an outlaw, I would have ye know that no honest man and true was ever harmed by me, and I take toll from none but the rich, the cruel, and the proud. Neither have I ever hurt the peasant folk, nor the husbandmen, nor the weak, nor the poor ones. But I chiefly hate the clergy, who in these days grow fat and rich upon poor men's lands, and from these I will have my dues, but only so that I may take from them and give to the needy. Now, sir, ye know what I am, and what my ways are. But come," his face cleared once more, "I am glad, since ye are the King's man, that we have met, Abbot. And since we have so met, why, ye must journey with me to Robin Hood's Inn, and we will see what fare the greenwood will provide for ye, and your followers, and for us all."

The abbot laughed again, but did not say him nay; and Robin, taking his horse's bridle once more, turned aside, whilst each of his men did likewise with the abbot's monks, and so the procession passed into the greenwood and through the trees to the forest lodge.

If the abbot felt any wonder at this turn of affairs, he did not say so, but, with his followers, dismounted from his horse meekly enough at the door of the lodge. Then, as they stood aside awkwardly, Robin bade his men lay a cloth upon the grass for dinner, and next instant glanced at his guests.

"I should not be using ye thus," he said severely,

and lifted a finger, "if ye had not been sent by His Majesty. Nay, more than that, I say, for the good King Richard's sake, not a penny will I take from any of ye, even though ye should have as much gold as ever I saw in my life."

As he spoke, he stepped proudly into the middle of the wide woodland glade, raising his bugle-horn to his lips, and next instant the old, long-drawn, sweet *"Come hither!"* thrice repeated, rang and rang again through the woods.

The monks stared, wondering what was coming; but in a moment they were staring more, and their jaws dropped open in astonishment, for into the glade, from all quarters of the forest, was pouring, a great crowd of men in green. Fast and thick they flocked in, armed with their bows, fine strong fellows and tall; and every man, as he came before Robin, knelt down and took off his cap, and so remained, humbly, until the outlaw chose to speak.

The abbot's blue eyes were full of wonder, and not a little envious, as he watched. Then he turned to one of his followers, a slim, black-eyed monk, who stood at his elbow.

"Oh, Faulk, Faulk!" he whispered. "What a fine sight is this—think'st thou not so? Methinks these fellows are humbler to their outlaw master than any of my lords and servants are to me. Here's a good lesson, then, that the court would do right well to learn from the woods."

Robin looked over his followers proudly.

"My merry men, Sir Priest!" he said cheerfully. "And now—to dinner!"

They sat down upon the grass before the outspread cloth of fine white linen, with its burden of good things. Fish there was, and wild-fowl, and deer's-flesh, and sweet wheaten bread, with foaming tankards of nut-brown ale and flagons of ruddy wine. All through the dinner, eaten merrily amidst the sweet forest scents beneath the great trees, the yellow-bearded abbot laughed and joked praised his meal and his host, and hugely enjoyed himself.

"Never was I feasted better, Master Robin," he declared; "nay, not at the King's own table! "

"Ah, the King!" Robin cried, and his brown face lit up with a look that warmed the abbot's heart. The outlaw sprang to hls feet as he spoke, lifting his flagon of ale high in the air.

"Take your cans, every man," he cried "and drink—a health unto His Majesty!"

And immediately monks and greencoats answered him, cheering, until the forest rang again:

"A health unto His Majesty!"

The abbot lifted the cup to his smiling lips and drank with the rest; then he set down his flagon and twinkled at the black-eyed Faulk beside him.

Now, after the dinner, the outlaws gave a show of their skill with quarter-staff and good yew-bow, and the abbot and his monks, watching and noting all, swore that Robin's men were finer in such practices than any they had ever seen. But Robin, laughing, declared that every man, shooting at the target and missing it, must take from him a box on the ear. Presently he took his bow himself, fitted a fine arrow, and made careful aim, but the wind turned his arrow aside, and it missed the mark, whereat monks and outlaws shouted, and the abbot cried:

"Hey, Master Robin! Take what ye have given, now. Come! A buffet o' the ear!"

And Robin, laughing again, answered: "By all means, Abbot. Will ye give it me?" and came close up, cap in hand. Then the abbot, doubling his fist, dealt him a sound blow upon the side of the head, so that the outlaw was sent sprawling.

"By my head, Abbot!" he cried, scrambling to his feet, "I think 'tis not often that a priest has so hard a hand as thou!"

The abbot's laugh rang out loud and merry as he helped the other up again.

"I like ye rarely, Master Robin," he said. "Now, tell me, if I could get your pardon from His Majesty the King, would ye receive it so? Would ye swear to be his follower—to serve him in everything, ye and your merry men?"

Robin's face lit up again, and his brown eyes flashed.

"With all my heart!" he cried in his great voice. And then, at a signal he gave, every outlaw whipped off his cap, and stood so, bareheaded, whilst the whole green-coated crew cried as with one voice:

"We swear to serve His Majesty with all our hearts, and to spend, if he so wills it, our last drop of blood for him."

Then the abbot stepped forward alone into the centre of the glade, looking round him with flushed face and shining eyes.

"My friends, I thank you, one and all," he said simply, and, as he spoke, threw back his hood, showing the fine head and noble countenance of Richard of England.

The outlaws stared, hardly understanding this strange turn of affairs; but Robin gave one look, and then fell upon his knee before the King's feet.

"Pardon, sire!" he murmured, very low. The King bent, took his hands, and set him on his feet again.

"Thou need'st not ask it, Robin," he said, very tenderly. "Nay, nay, stand up, my friend. What hast thou to fear, and who shall speak against Richard when he pardons Robin Hood and Robin Hood's brave fellows, every one?"

And next instant the woods of Sherwood were echoing and ringing from end to end with the sound of the merry men's cheering.

* * * *

So it came to pass that after a few more days of festival in the town, the King and his courtiers, with Robin Hood and his greencoats, set out for London town, rejoicing. And at court the outlaws stayed, serving their king faithfully and well.

19

Robin Hood at the Court of King Richard

The men of Robin Hood's band who went with him to Londcn expected to live a life of ease and plenty whilst in the King's service.

"We shall have a place to live in, plenty of food, and regular wages," they said. What more could they want?

They had not been at the King's court long before they saw how wrong they had been. When Robin applied for money to pay the wages of his men, he was told that he would be expected to pay them himself.

"All the nobles do it," explained one knight, "and so do the knights. If a man is too poor to pay his men then he has no right to be here at all!"

Robin had brought with him a tremendous chest filled with gold coins. He was able to pay his men their proper wages from it. Yet he knew that the gold would not last for ever. He soon learnt that few of the knights paid their men anything at all.

Robin was lighthearted and happy at first. He paid his men their wages, and was free with his money. Other knights took advantage of his happy-go-lucky spirit to borrow from him.

"Robin Hood," one would say, "I am short of money. I want to pay my men, who are beginning to grumble.

I beg you to lend me enough to pay them, or there will be trouble amongst them."

Robin always was kind hearted. He knew, also, that there might come a day when he would need the friendship of the knights. So he gave them money from his chest.

"I'm beginning to see the wood at the bottom of the chest," he murmured to himself one day. "It will not be long before the chest is empty."

His words came true. There came a day when he had no money left. Now would be his chance, he thought, to borrow back from the many knights who had so long been borrowing from him. He asked some of them to repay their debts. None could. Knights who were once his best friends now spurned him. With money, Robin found that everyone was his friend. Without it only his old comrades stood loyally by him.

He called all his men to him and told them honestly of the state of affairs. They were sympathetic, but they could not live without pay, and before long most of them left the court and returned to their homes. Once there, they found the attraction of their old forest habits too strong for them, and they lived once more under the greenwood trees.

Robin Hood bore the life at court as long as he could. Few friends were with him now. He was lonely. He talked to Maid Marian of his great urge to return to Sherwood Forest. Marian knew that he would never be happy away from his beloved greenwood, so she said that she was willing to return to the forest with him.

"You must first ask the King, Robin," she said. "He

would never forgive you if you left without his permission."

"I will," agreed Robin.

He sought permission from the King's Chamberlain to see the King. When he was at last admitted to the royal presence, he told of the hunger in his heart to see the greenwood once more.

"It is a kind of homesickness, sire," said Robin. "Until I have again seen my greenwood home, and until I have stayed there for a time, I'm sure I shall not be able to settle down to anything."

The King considered Robin's plea for a moment.

"H'm!" he murmured, after a short silence. "I think there *is* something in what you say, Robin Hood. He was a just man and he knew that Robin would be of little use to him in his present state of mind. A refreshing visit to his greenwood home might work wonders. I will grant you your wish," he said at length. "You may visit Sherwood Forest again, but you must return to me in two weeks' time. Not a day longer than that must you stay."

Robin left the King's room in a happy frame of mind. He ran straight to Maid Marian and told her the good news. He left for Sherwood Forest that day, arranging for Maid Marian to follow a week later by horse and wagon. She could never have undertaken the journey on foot, and Robin found that no one could be persuaded to start out in less than a week. Thus he set out alone on the long journey.

20

Robin's Return to the Greenwood

Midge-the-Miller's son was now in charge of his mill, for his father had died and left it to him. He was out of touch with the outlaws who had not gone with Robin Hood to London. His only link with the happy past was Friar Tuck.

Every Sunday, Friar Tuck and he would meet and stroll into the greenwood.

On one of these walks, when both were feeling a little sad, Midge-the-Miller's son turned suddenly to the friar.

"Did you hear a sound?" he asked, excitedly.

"No," said Friar Tuck. "What sound was it?"

"Perhaps it was nothing."

"I have heard that some of the folk are back in the forest," said Friar Tuck.

"What sort of folk do you mean?"

"Our sort," said the Friar. He corrected himself, "I mean, the sinful sort we once were."

"There it is again," said the other, interrupting him.

There was no doubt about the noise this time. It was the old call of the horn that once they knew so well.

The two ran in the direction of the sound. What they would meet they knew not. They hoped desperately that, by some amazing stroke of good fortune, they would meet their old master again.

Soon they came to a small opening amongst the trees, where three men were grouped. One of them was bending over another, who was lying on the ground. He appeared to be exhausted. The third was a giant in size. As soon as he saw Midge-the-Miller's son and Friar Tuck coming towards him he drew a knife from his belt.

Friar Tuck recognised the man at once.

"Put away your knife, Little John," he called. "Do you not remember us? We are your old companions, Friar Tuck and Midge-the-Miller's son."

Little John was happy indeed to see his old friends once more.

"Who's with you?" asked the friar.

"The one bending down," said Little John, "is Will Scarlet. Surely he has not changed so much that you fail to recognise him?"

"And who is that on the ground?" asked Midge-the-Miller's son as they walked nearer to the figure.

"The captain!" whispered Will Scarlet, turning from the prostrate form of Robin.

Friar Tuck ran forward to his old master.

"Robin! Sweet Robin!" he cried. "Look up, my master! You remember your old chaplain!"

Robin pulled himself up. After walking all the way from London, with hardly a scrap to eat, he was weak and almost worn out. It had been a hard, four-days' journey. He would never have completed it if he had not been so determined to see the friendly forest once again. Now that he was back in the greenwood he knew that he would soon recover.

"It is grand to see you," he said to Friar Tuck and Midge-the-Miller's son. "I have been given only fourteen days' leave from the King to visit my forest haunts, and the days will soon pass, I fear."

With a sudden effort, Robin stood on his feet. He placed his horn to his lips. The old familiar call rang out through the forest. Figures streaked through the greenwood towards them. Presently a crowd of Robin's old outlaws were gathered round him once more.

Robin put away his horn, and looked happily at his old comrades. Already he felt his old spirit and joy of life returning. Many of the outlaws facing him had joined him when he left Nottingham to serve the King, but one by one they had left the King's service to go back to Sherwood Forest. This was the life they knew and loved; this was where their hearts lay.

"Welcome! Welcome, my old friends!" cried Robin. "I have come again to shoot the King's deer—but only for a short time."

Little John and Will Scarlet sat together that evening. Robin Hood had gone to bed early, for he was still very tired.

"Our master must stay with us," said Little John. "He needs us just as much as we need him."

"He will never go back on his word to the King," said Will Scarlet.

"But if he were held here by force he would not be able to keep his promise, would he?" grinned Little John.

"What do you mean?"

"Supposing you and I bound him and held him prisoner! He couldn't possibly return."

Little John was in earnest. He knew where his master's heart lay. He also knew that it would only be by force that Robin would be persuaded to stay in his forest home, instead of obeying the King's command to return after fourteen days.

Together Little John and Will Scarlet worked out a plan to capture Robin and hold him captive, until one of them had visited the King and explained how dear to Robin Hood was his life in the forest.

The plan was complete by the time Robin was due to start back on his long journey to London. Maid Marian had joined him some days before, and she had been told by Little John of what was afoot. She kept silent about it until the day of Robin's departure.

As he was making ready to leave the camp, Little John and Will Scarlet pounced on him from behind. Robin was unprepared, and could not understand the meaning of the outrage. He was even more mystified when he found himself tightly secured with stout ropes.

Little John stepped in front of him.

"Forgive us, master," he said apologetically. "We know that you will not stay of your own free will. We know, too, that your heart lies here in the greenwood. So we are holding you captive until a messenger returns from the King to tell us his views."

Robin was furious at the trick that had been played on him, but he was powerless to act.

Will Scarlet left that day for London. He was gone a week. On his return from the King of England, he called Little John to him, and together they reported to Robin.

"Master," said Will, smiling. "I explained to the King

that you were held captive by your own men. I told him that this was your true home and that you could never be happy at court. I begged him to allow you to stay here with us. The King listened to all I had to say. Then, after a long silence, he replied that you could stay in Sherwood Forest on condition that you and all the Merrie Men would be at his service, if ever the country was in danger. I gave him that assurance."

"You mean, I am free to stay?" asked Robin, incredulously.

"Yes, master," answered Will Scarlet joyfully. "Let us live again the life of adventure that we once loved so well."

Robin was overjoyed at the news. So was Little John. All the outlaws in the forest were summoned to the camp, and they made a great feast under the trees to celebrate Robin Hood's return to the old life of freedom and adventure in the greenwood.

21

Robin's Death and Burial

Winter had come to the forest, and all the broad glades and long aisles of the woodlands were brown and damp and still. The trees, stripped of their fresh summer greenery, seemed dismally bare, whilst all the ground beneath them was strewn with a brown and yellow carpet of fallen leaves. Save the gentle moaning of the wind through the branches, and, now and then, the sad piping of a distant robin, the woods were silent. Birds and beasts had mostly fled—to seek the snug shelter of their winter homes, or the fair skies and gentle air of warmer, sunnier lands.

Down one of the damp, leaf-strewn paths of the forest two men were walking slowly in the fading light of the afternoon. Both were clad as foresters and carried their great bows, but one, at whose waist hung a silver-mounted bugle-horn, leaned heavily upon his taller companion, and seemed to walk with difficulty. The other helped him tenderly, and from time to time spoke some cheerful word as they passed slowly along.

"Courage, master! "he said once as his comrade came to a standstill, and, breathing painfully, pressed one hand to his side. "Courage! Can ye go but a little farther? We are not so far from the lodge."

"I will try, John," answered the other, who was Robin Hood, "I will try, but 'tis this deadly sickness

He swayed a little as he spoke, and then sat down suddenly upon the trunk of a fallen tree that lay near. "Fetch me water from yonder stream," he whispered, with lips as pale as death, and Little John flew to do his bidding, and brought him some of the cold spring water in his cap.

Robin drank quickly, and presently seemed to revive, although all the fresh colour had fled from his once brown cheeks. Then his eye fell upon the big bow at his feet, and he looked up at John with a little smile.

"What shootings we have had, John, and what merry times, with these good yew-bows of ours," he said; "but," with a sigh, "I shall shoot no more, I fear me, in merry Sherwood, for my arm has lost its power, now, and my arrows will not fly as they were wont to do."

His tone was low and sorrowful, and Little John, looking at the thin wasted figure and the brave face drawn with pain, could not answer for a moment. Presently Robin got slowly to his feet, and, as he did so, gave a feeble laugh.

"Faith!" he said, "my legs seem to belong to some other person, they are so weak." Then he looked round and a thought seemed to strike him. "We are more than a league from our lodge, John, and I—I—do not think I can walk there, but see, we are near to Kirkley Hall, where a cousin of mine lives—she is the mistress of the house. I have heard many a time that she hath much skill in curing ailments by bleeding the sufferer, and so I will go thither and she shall bleed me. Will ye help me there, my friend? It is but a walk of ten minutes, I think."

Little John, cheered at his master's more hopeful tone, agreed heartily, and they set forth once more through the forest.

In a quarter of an hour—for the sick man could walk only slowly—they came in sight of Kirkley Hall, a long, low, dark building of stone, with deep-set, tiny windows, and with the forest-trees growing up almost to its very doors.

As they came up to the entrance a woman's face, which John had noticed at one of the small casements watching them approach, vanished suddenly, and the outlaw shivered with a quick sense of distrust and fear.

"I do not like this place, and it seems to give you a cold welcome, master," he said, as Robin, leaning against the door-post heavily, pulled at the bell-rope.

In a moment the door was opened, and the woman whom John had seen at the window stood before them. She wore a long grey gown that fell in straight folds to her feet; her black hair was put back smoothly under her head-dress, but her dark eyes were narrow and cunning, and her lips were tightly pressed and thin. She held a lamp in her hand, for it was now almost dusk.

"Cousin," said Robin at once, "I am very ill, I fear me, and I want you to bleed me, and, if you can, to cure me. I cannot tell what is ailing me, but I am very weak."

The woman's thin lips broke into a smile, which she tried in vain to make pleasant. She held the lamp up higher.

"What, Robin!" she cried. "Is it my cousin, Robin Hood? Oh come in, come in, I pray ye. Alas, poor fellow, how weak ye seem! How long have ye been thus? Indeed, I will gladly do what I can. Come in!"

She stretched out one hand and drew the sick man gently indoors, but when Little John would have stepped after him, she stopped him with a look.

"There is no room in the house for any of your followers, cousin," she said coldly.

Robin lifted his head with an effort. "I am sorry, John," he said, "but ye hear what my cousin says. I will come to ye again when she has bled me. It is better that ye should go back to the woods."

"I will obey you, Master Robin," replied John, and turned away from the door, but as he did so he muttered to himself: "though I will keep in sight of Kirkley Hall until you come forth again, for I like neither the house nor its mistress."

The woman stood at the door a moment, watching his figure grow smaller in the distance between the trees. Then she turned to Robin.

"Come, my cousin," she said in her smooth tones; "I will take ye to a chamber where ye may rest, and there I will bleed ye."

She led him slowly along a dark passage and up a twisting flight of stone steps that ended in a heavy door in the wall. This she threw open, showing a small, low, stone-walled chamber with one tiny window, through which the last rays of daylight crept dully. Under the window was a low couch, but, save this, there was no other furniture in the room.

The woman helped Robin on to the rough pallet, and then, after stripping him of his coat, left the chamber for an instant, to return presently with a basin. She crossed the room, knelt down beside him, and, baring his right arm, opened a vein in it with a small instrument that she drew from the bosom of her gown.

The blood flowed freely, and Robin, white-lipped, closed his eyes and lay back.

The woman rose from her knees softly and went towards the door, her eyes upon his face.

"You will be better soon, my cousin," she said coolly, and with that passed out of the room, locking the door behind her.

But the sick man took no heed of her words; he did not hear them, for he had fainted as she closed the door upon him and left him alone.

Outside, the mistress of Kirkley Hall stood for a moment on the stairs and laughed under her breath.

"So shall you die," she whispered, "Robin Hood of Sherwood, robber and outlaw, master of five hundred merry men. Aye, so shall you die, alone and unaided—die at my hands; for I have ever hated you, and there are many who will praise me and reward me for what I have done but now. Farewell, then. You shall use your bow no more, nor blow your horn, neither shall your men of the forest, nor the forest itself, ever know you again. Farewell!"

So she left the locked door behind her, and passed down the stairs.

When Robin came to himself once more, a watery moon was shining through the narrow window, and he could see the woods below, all black and still. The blood was still flowing from his arm; he felt weak and cold, and his mouth was parched and dry.

"My cousin is long in returning," he murmured, and

lay still. He wondered where she was and where John was, but he did not rise from the couch. Doubtless it was good for his arm to bleed so. His cousin must know. But he wished she had not left him alone. His mind wandered to many things after that, and presently he slipped into a heavy sleep in spite of the pain. From some distant castle tower a clock chimed the hours, one after another, and an owl hooted dismally from the woods, but no one came near the locked chamber. Robin woke and shivered, and wondered a little, and slept again. Still the blood flowed steadily and slowly from his arm. Dawn came then broad daylight, and still no one came to help him. How long the hours were!

At last the thought flashed upon him that no one would ever come; that his cousin had meant to open the vein in his arm, and then leave him to bleed to death. But why? "I never harmed her," thought Robin, and lay pondering, white and weak, upon his rough bed. Another hour passed. His strength was ebbing fast, but a sudden desire seized him to get free, to get away from Kirkley Hall, back into the forest, if it was only to die there. Painfully he lifted himself up, crawled across the room, and shook the door. It was fast. He dragged himself to the window and looked down. Alas! it was too small to squeeze through, and, even had it not been so, the ground was twenty feet below, and he was too weak to leap now.

He sank back panting, then again his dull eyes lit up and his feeble hand groped at his waist. There was his bugle-horn—and there was John. John had always come at his call; he would not fail him now.

He lifted the horn in one trembling hand. "'Tis the last summons thou wilt ever sound for me, old friend," he said, and set it to his lips.

* * * *

"Come hither! Come hither!"

Little John, sitting with his back against a tree-trunk in the forest, gloomily watching the windows of Kirkley Hall, started to his feet and listened. The notes of that horn were feeble and wavering, but he knew the sound well. How often, upon joyous May mornings long ago, had his master's sturdy blast wakened the echoes in Sherwood's glades! He listened again. *"Come hither!"* The horn was sounding a third time, but fainter, as if the breath of him who blew it was failing fast.

"He wants me!" cried John. "He is worse than he was—perhaps dying. Ah! That evil house—that evil woman!"

He was dashing through the trees as he spoke, and, coming up to the hall, rushed at the door without stopping to knock at it. It gave way before his great strength, and, finding himself inside, he sped down the first passage he saw and up a flight of twisting steps, where a locked door faced him. From the other side a faint voice was calling "John! John!"

"I am coming, master!" Little John replied. Gathering himself for one mighty effort, he hurled himself with all his strength at the door. It crashed open, and Robin Hood, as he saw his man, lifted his head and tried to smile.

"John," he whispered, "John, she has bled me——"

"To death!" ended John fiercely, and crossing the room, took his master in his strong arms. But Robin had fainted once more.

He was roused again presently by the other holding a little flask of wine to his lips.

"Drink," said John, "and afterwards grant me one wish, master."

The dying, man drank greedily, and then, a little refreshed, asked, "What is your wish, John?"

The other's eyes flashed, and Robin, as he lay in his arms, felt his great body quiver with passion. "Give me leave," he cried, "to set fire to Kirkley Hall and all within it; let me burn house and servants and mistress to the ground!"

Robin held up a feeble hand.

"No, no, John," he whispered; "I cannot grant ye that. Never in all my life have I hurt a woman, and I will not do so now, nor will I see it done. Leave them alone, John. Neither you nor I must punish them." He paused a moment, and then said: "I think I am going fast. Lift me up to the window, and give me my bow and an arrow."

The other obeyed him, and so, held in John's arms, Robin fitted his arrow and then turned his brown eyes again upon his friend's face.

"'Tis my last one," he said with a little smile, "and where it drops, there dig my grave and let me be buried. Put a green sod at my head, John, and another at my feet, and let my bow be laid beside me, for it has ever been my true friend. And mark my grave, so that all men may say as they pass by it, 'There lies bold

Robin Hood of Sherwood'."

His tones grew fainter, and John, with a catch in his voice, promised to do all as he had said. Then Robin lifted himself up and drew his bow, sending the arrow speeding out of the window, and watched it take its flight over the trees and drop down suddenly into their brown depths.

But that last effort had been too much for him, for his strength gave way next instant as his companion's arms tightened their hold, and turning his face to Little John's he fell dead against the other's shoulder.

They found his last arrow beneath a tree in the woods, and in that spot they buried him as he had bidden them, with a green sod at his head and another at his feet, and his good bow beside him.

And as the forest had been his beloved home in the days of his joyous life, so in death it was, even as he had willed it his last resting-place.

Dear Shireen,
I hope you enjoyed reading the book, it is a real nice story.

From:
your friend
forever
Davina